THE EARTH
EXPERIMENT

PATRICK VAITUS

THE EARTH EXPERIMENT

iUniverse books may be ordered through booksellers or by contacting:

iUniverse
1663 Liberty Drive
Bloomington, IN 47403
www.iuniverse.com
844-349-9409

Because of the dynamic nature of the Internet, any web addresses or links contained in this book may have changed since publication and may no longer be valid. The views expressed in this work are solely those of the author and do not necessarily reflect the views of the publisher, and the publisher hereby disclaims any responsibility for them.

Any people depicted in stock imagery provided by Getty Images are models, and such images are being used for illustrative purposes only. Certain stock imagery © Getty Images.

ISBN: 978-1-6632-5295-1 (sc)
ISBN: 978-1-6632-5296-8 (e)

Library of Congress Control Number: 2023908542

Print information available on the last page.

iUniverse rev. date: 05/09/2023

To see the main characters list and details check the last page

CHAPTER 1

The intergalactic hyper fly

As we live an eternity, we have to focus on doing right things.

Dem, The official journal

Zeu and Herr decided to inspect the navigation room of the ship.

"It's unbelievable," Herr said, "we've been on this ship for such a long time and yet we've never been in the navigation room."

"Irrelevant!" Zeu answered. "We know every detail of every corner, of every piece of equipment, of every cable, and all connections with all the software through the microchip implanted in our brain. It is connected with all ship's computers and …

"I know," Herr interrupted him. "But still, it's different when you see it in reality. It's better than holographic or mnemonic projection. Especially for us …" she looked seriously at him and with her accent on the last two words,

"... eternal entities." She smiled broadly at him, but Zeu appeared not to enjoy her joke very much.

Today for some reason he was enjoying admiring his muscular body much more than on any other day. His muscles where more developed than the muscles of the other men on the ship. *With only one exception ... Cronn*, it was like an echo in his mind. His hair was long, past his shoulders and flowing like a black river. His skin was also different from the others, somehow he looked more tanned. His eyes were black, blacker than anyone on the ship. His medium long beard, matched by his hair, was carefully maintained. He was able to maintain his peak physical appearance through a series of exercises carefully developed over many years, and particularly by ingesting only selected foods and proteins. The specific antiaging ingredients of the food made Zeu, Herr and all the others immortal.

Think of it as an opportunity to reinvent yourself, Zeu thought. And Herr was, as always with him. He had always wondered why she liked him so much. She joined him at the gym whenever he went there, and imitated his exercise regime, but at a lower level. As a result, her wonderful body was perhaps a bit too muscled for a woman. Her skin was white. Her hair was almost as black as his, but just a little longer and curly. She was tall, but just a bit shorter than him. They made a perfect couple.

After a short silence, Herr spoke, "Remember, I don't like to be contradicted," she said smiling bitterly at him."

Zeu looked intently at her, and despite the fact that his telepathic message might be received, he replied, "you'd better get used to this, especially if we want our plan to succeed."

"Do you understand why this project is called 'the earth experiment'?" Herr asked him somewhat vaguely.

"Yes, because it is an experiment done on a planetary scale," he answered, quite convinced.

"That would just be terraforming then. Every terraforming project that our civilization has done was an experiment on a planetary scale," Herr was unsatisfied with his answer.

"The difference is that we will start with a totally inorganic planet, and our interventions are limited compared to classical terraforming," Zeu did his best to convince her.

"Any interventions we make will be terraforming, more or less." Herr was still firm on her position.

"Once we get there, the planet will be under total quarantine. All the meteors that contain any trace of organics will be deflected away from the planet. We want to create life from inorganics on that planet. If you need more details on the program you can access the schedule data at …"

"I know, I know …" she interrupted, bored by his explanations. "In a way, it's like we'll be discovering our own organic evolution."

As the door of the elevator began to open, he felt a terrible verge to kiss her. Sensing his impulse, Herr said, "Do not kiss me here and now."

"Why? "

"Because, it is strictly forbidden."

"No, it's not forbidden. It's only recommended."

"In any case," she appeared unconvinced, "why don't you have your computer create a replica of me, if you haven't already yet, and use it for all your perverse pleasures."

"I already did. I'd imagine you have a replica of me as well," he grinned.

"You've made no secret of your sexual passions. I'd wager that several of the other women on the ship have a replica of you as well."

"As you said, regarding the navigation room, reality is different than a simulation. A replica is not as good as the original."

As they stepped out of elevator, Herr stopped and turned to him. "A replica is better than the original. It is created especially for this purpose. It is perfection!" She paused, giving him some time to let it sink in. "Now, let's focus on the current matter, this navigation room, as we are already here?" she smiled feeling like she had won a small victory, and turned back to the impressive navigation room.

Three people stood there. Two of them were focused on a complicated holographic protection of some communication satellites and the nearby stars and planets. Watching over them stood a tall and unusually slim lady. She was watching the holographic projection, or was she supervising them? She wore a black dress that was very tight to her body, making her appear much taller than she was. Her hair was very short cut. Her tight clothing and short hair made her appear too skinny.

"That is Discordia," Herr said to Zeu in a very low voice. "It is said that she and her crew are the oldest ones on the ship. They are the first generation to enjoy the benefit of the eternal life extension."

"I've heard that too," Zeu answered, "they were among the first batches of people who started the life extension program. At that time, the technology wasn't very well-known and was quite risky because of its side effects."

"Yes, at the very beginning there were some side effects. I've studied this in detail. It is no longer a concern, now that we are eating the right proteins." For a few moments they were silent as they walked slowly, carefully analyzing the impressive navigation room. It was quite large but not at all as large as the main control room, or the main auditorium, or the main living space of the ship. It was rather comparable in dimensions to a large meeting room. The navigation room was very well organized with navigation computers, spaces for holographic projections, chairs with interesting shapes. Herr always felt the need to deliver information to Zeu, even though she was sure he knew all the information and was able to search for any information in the computer's databases in real time, through his microchip brain implant.

"Now we are flying at hyper-light speed, and yet we maintain a stable equilibrium. When the ship is accelerating or decelerating, the navigation room staff sit in these chairs, and they are rigidly secured and shielded from the forces of our momentum."

"Can you believe, after millennia of science and evolution, we are still quite rudimentary on space navigation technology?" Herm, said in a sad voice. He materialized near them using the ship's teleportation system.

"I would agree with you Herm," Herr said in a polite yet imperious voice, "but maybe there are real limits. We should admit that in some areas, we have reached the absolute maximum. Beyond that maximum threshold, nothing more can be achieved. Anything more is impossible. The maximum in inter-galactic travel has been achieved, and we must accept it."

Disturbed by Herr's observation, Herm raised his blue eyes toward her. He looked for a moment at her and at Zeu. Zeu and Herr returned his gaze. He was much younger then Zeu and quite skinny. He had nice muscles. His delicate features dissolved into a smile that he directed at Herr.

"You may be right Herr, as disturbing as it is. Despite the fact that we are able to use hyper-light speed, space folding, and so on, we still cannot fly directly from point A to point B when they are situated in faraway galaxies, as is the case now."

Zeu smiled, "but once we reach point B, we will be able to communicate instantaneously with our home planet, and send matter and even life forms back to them."

"And all this will be possible," Herr completed Zeu's sentence, "because of the star gates we will sprinkle in our wake along our way."

Zeu put his hand on Herm's shoulder in a friendly gesture, "history is going to remember your name my friend, because you are the pilot of this mission. Without you all this would not be possible." Herr also looked at Herm with admiration.

Herm was not convinced. He knew all the main crew leaders, with their extremely long lifespans, had achieved sufficient piloting skills. Second, this ship was in fact like a living being. It was totally automated, with nano-computers and real brains implanted in the key control and command loops. He was about to respond but changed his mind, thinking *some recognition is always welcome*; also he heard Discordia approaching. She was deliberately stomping in an effort to catch the attention of the three leaders. She always wanted them to realize her primary importance on the ship's crew. *How unique I am,* she thought proudly.

Adjusting her tiny voice to make it sound more gravely, she said, "So sorry to disturb you sir, but I have important developments to report." She paused to give the three leaders time to focus on her. Proud of herself, Discordia continued, "We just lunched the group of 10,913 star gate devices. We have received their signals, and have confirmed that they are all fully operational."

With a smile Herm said, "thanks so much Discordia. Your skills and supervision are greatly appreciated."

Trying to make Discordia feel appreciated, and despite the fact that they all knew the answer, Herr asked, "are we on schedule Discordia?"

With a victorious smile Discordia said, "We are on track ma'am, I've supervised everything very carefully."

———◆———

Atena had no idea why Afronda had invited her to the ship's garden, but as she waited for her to arrive, she was filled with admiration for the beautiful garden. Strictly speaking, the garden was too large for a star ship's garden. It produced absolutely no food as food they needed was produced trough complicated chemical synthesis. Also, the oxygen generated by the garded was quite insignificant compared to what was produced in the algae containers. From this point of view, Atena repeatedly asked herself whether the architects and designers had been right to waste so much useful space on the star ship for a garden.

"But it is beautiful", Afronda would always argue. "And

real", Herr would usually add. Still, Atena was not totally convinced that using such an enormous space in a star ship was a good idea. *It looks to me like a waste of space,* she had explained once to Zeu. *And it's not just what we see here; behind these walls are complicated mechanisms to protect this huge garden from the incredible forces the ship undergoes during acceleration and deceleration to hyper-light speed, space folding, and so on*

"It is a huge garden, but I like it," Zeu said to her once. "Atena, you should see the good in things: the atmosphere in the garden is so calm, you can recover nicely here and make plans for attack."

It wasn't long before Atena stopped arguing with the others on the subject of the garden. It seemed like all were against her, *and it's not a good strategy to continue in that kind of situation,* she reminded herself.

A river wound its way through the middle of the garden and ended in a lively cascade that was flowed down into a large lake. Atena walked on a bolted bridge that curved artfully over. She looked down to the water of the late. It was so clear. There was a very interesting selection of water plants harmoniously distributed within the lake. On the surface other aquatic plans with wonderful flowers floated.

As though looking in a mirror, Atena could see the reflection of her beautiful face on the still surface of the lake. Her face was indeed perfect. White skin, long black hair that was just a little bit curly. She carefully observed her body as well. It was also wonderful. *However,* she thought, *I am perhaps a little bit too muscular for a woman.* Atena undertook huge metabolic efforts to keep her muscle mass down, but it was very difficult, especially for someone with her fighting skills.

I am an experimented fighter, but I like to look feminine too, she thought. She recalled how much she had hated Afronda at their first beauty class meeting. Afronda had been unable to stop herself from saying: "Oh dear, you have to get rid of these masculine muscles immediately. I am sure you still love your femininity." At that time Atena hadn't agreed, but in time she understood Afronda's point: *beauty matters.*

"The whole universe oriented to beauty, to lovely forms; and you should too, Atena', Afronda had said. An eternity had passed between Afronda's early lessons and today. Now they were good friends, although sometimes Atena still felt jealous of Afronda. *She has everything, all thanks to her beauty. She can successfully manipulate both men and women. Afronda's body is the benchmark of beauty. Her skin is quite possibly the perfect shade of white in the entire known universe. Her eyes are so blue, her face so unbelievably perfect. And her blond curly hair…*

For a moment Atena toyed with the idea of changing her black hair to blond, but she immediately discarded the idea. *Afronda will think I'm trying to copy her. And since her lessons, I have evolved.* Athena felt a little nervous, she was running out of time and wasn't sure her wonderful dress was perfectly arranged on her body. She let the home robots do their job. She had let them work even a little longer than the usual. She wanted to be perfect for this meeting. Afronda paid so much attention to details. As Afronda was always perfectly dressed and arranged, she expects that from all the crew members. No exception!

Afronda's invitation was strange and confusing, "*we have to meet as soon as possible*", nothing more. It was not at all her style. Unless something urgent was indeed coming up … *But what could be so urgent?* Atena asked herself. She ran through the possibilities in her mind, searching for a hypothesis. She had even asked the computers to run scenarios, however nothing conclusive had come up. Atena was certainly intrigued.

The intensive mental effort of running through possible scenarios caused her heartbeat to quicken. She tried to calm herself down by looking at the beautiful flowers around the lake. She was now at the apex of the curved bridge and she could see almost the entire garden from her vantage point. Suddenly, she stopped admiring the garden as she felt Afronda approaching.

There was something very wrong indeed. Afronda approached with a strange expression on her face. Thanks to her education and her abilities, Atena understood that it was not a charade. Afronda was genuinely upset. Usually, Afronda enjoyed admiring the garden so much, but now she walked directly to Atena and paid absolutely no attention to the beauty of her surroundings.

"Dear Atena, I cannot explain to you how much I appreciate you accepting my invitation", Afronda said with a grateful smile. Her smile was a balance between sadness and happiness, with a note of disappointment that *you might be not be able to help me* and *you are my only hope*. Atena was always amazed at Afronda's ability to evoke emotions in others with nothing more than a look, and she was always willing to learn more.

"It is my pleasure, dear Afronda, but what's bothering you? I can feel your anxiety."

"Indeed. Something is very wrong. I have a strange feeling that something terrible is going to happen soon and I need your help to prevent it." She paused, gazing Atena with her blue eyes that instantly transformed to red as they were flooded with blood, reflecting danger nearby. Atena was amazed at her ability to transform. Just a second ago her look had been so shiny, and now it was so tragic.

"But what are you looking to defeat? What are we fighting? What kind of help do you need?"

"I … I have a strange feeling."

"Based on what?"

"On a premonition."

Atena stopped for a moment. She made a huge effort to return her breath to normal. At the same time, through her mental microchip link, she checked the database for records on Afronda's premonition abilities. She was very surprised to find that indeed there were some notes. Quite vague, but enough for a totally logically-orientated mind like Aetna's to understand there was something serious going on here.

"I'm sorry to disturb you Atena, but I have no one else to talk to about this."

"What are you saying? You have the people on your team. You are their leader. They adore you."

"They are not able to protect me against this danger." Afronda said sharply.

"All the other leaders here on the ship love you."

"They are in danger too."

Again Atena had to make an effort to slow down her breathing.

As if giving Atena time to recover, Afronda continued "and my best friend Gee: she is in cryogenic hibernation. I don't understand why she chose to travel in stasis. I told her cryogenic technology has a negative impact on skin cells."

"I don't know about that. It's a very stable technology. We've been using it for thousands of years and it has proven no side effects."

"That doesn't matter," Afronda shot back. "Gee is my true friend. Why would she leave me alone? Why would she decide to hibernate now?"

"Because Uran is hibernating too. They're always together."

For a moment Afronda drifted off into a daydream, *like Zeu and Herr,* she thought.

Atena made a serious face, "and how exactly can I help you?"

"Teach me to fight!"

Atena was shocked again. She adjusted her breathing. She intended to hide the fact that Afronda was surprising her at every turn.

"To fight? With laser guns? Or mental weapons? You'd be better off asking Arr."

"I might ask him too. However, I am expecting a physical fight first, and I believe you are the best person on the ship to teach me."

"But the training will change your body, your muscle tone and..."

"I don't care. That is a minor consideration, I am a superior character." After a short pause, Afronda said firmly. "This is an emergency. My life depends on it."

Atena felt a strange sensation on her skin.

Dem and Hest had been inspecting the ship's living quarter for more than four hours. Because the living quarters were quite gigantic, accessing them through the stairs required an enormous effort, so they used the high-speed elevators instead. Finally they decided to take a break. They rested in the living room of a condo unit and commanded the house robot to bring them some refreshing drinks.

Dem was a rather mature lady, medium to tall, with a beautiful face and beautiful black hair with a few white threads visible.

Hest always wondered how Dem (or her computers) managed this mature look. She had noticed that the current protein complex made it quite easy to maintain the appearance of youth, but it was difficult to show some age, because just a few drops of the medicine and all signs of age vanished.

In contrast to Dem, Hest was a young woman. Extremely beautiful, though somewhat shorter than Dem. Hest hated the discrepancy in height between the two of them, because they were always together and being compared to one another, and being taller, Dem appeared to be the leader. But from the very beginning, the regulations of the mission stated that they were absolutely equal.

Now I must always act in the front of everyone to prove that she is not my leader, Hest thought.

"I have to admit the living quarters are huge," Dem said, taking a large sip from her refreshing drink.

"What do you expect? Our experiment is huge too," Hest said, philosophically smiling at Dem.

"Are you referring to their experiment, or to our experiment?"

"Ours. But I think it would be a gross error not to keep a close eye on theirs too. Don't you think so?"

Dem was enjoying her refreshing drink so much she forgot to answer. Finally she responded, "Yes of course. First we should provide individuals to replace any of them at any moment."

"Right now we're not able to do it," Hest answered in a bitter tone.

"I know, but this mission is in its very beginning stage. I expect there will be no need to replace one at this point." Dem said convinced.

"I still don't like it!" Hest answered.

"Let's start our experiment immediately. These massive living quarters need to be populated," Dem said smiling widely, "and we have more than enough DNA for this. I'm always so excited about trying to predict the psychology of new human beings based on their DNA and the mathematical combinations of their genes."

"I disagree," Hest said emphasizing her words, "that cannot be 100% correct. However, as long as we are up to 50% we are doing well enough. The other 50% can be achieved with the proper education and training of the individuals."

"You are indeed correct. We need to create a strong leader in the first group of individuals."

"We agreed to that, but we didn't agree on the right

DNA combination. We have to exercise immense caution. Our actions could create grave consequences."

"Until now, we have collected an impressive collection of reproductive cells from the current seniors of this expedition. They really like to play with their replicas, and we've been able to harvest a lot of DNA from their genital organs.

"But at this moment, none of those cells are involved in our experiment."

"True. But sometimes I feel like we are too limited by the Natural Being Law. We are required by this law to create life strictly from the original being's cells. We have enough technology to modify their DNA to obtain the right individuals for our own proposes."

"Or superior individuals."

They examined each other for a while, trying to read each other's thoughts. Then, smiling at Hest Dem said, "I won't ever contravene the law."

"But what if we are completely isolated and we need these mathematically-projected individuals?" Hest wondered.

"That will never happen on this expedition. We have the SG – star gate devices – that will connect us instantly with our planet of origin."

"If the SG devices work properly, the Natural Being Law will be in place and enforceable."

"And if they don't …"

Hest and Dem nodded almost in unison and took a large sip from their drinks. This unspoken possibility opened a strange door.

Apoll was closely watching the crew that was working around one of the huge star gate devices. There were a few people and many robots. The complicated star gate's electronics were covered by an alloy that appeared to be a perfect mirror. As Apoll approached the star gate device, he admired his wonderful body on the gate's reflective surface. He paused to reflect that if Afronda's body was the standard for female beauty, then his own body was the standard for male beauty.

His body was so well developed, nice muscles, beautiful white skin, long yellow curly hair, and clear blue eyes. The white collar was tight on his body, making him look awesome.

The few males from his team copied him almost in everything, the way he dressed, the way he wore his hair, even his gestures. His team was an example of harmony for all the other leaders and their teams.

A few parts of the star gate device were uncovered by the protective alloy enclosure and Apoll focused his attention on the electronic equipment. The robots worked intensely. The few beautiful human males gave instructions to the robots from time to time, while discreetly looking at Apoll and offering him short smiles.

Quite satisfied the status of the star gate device, he decided to return to his cubicle. When he got there, he was upset to see Heff. It was his bad luck to share his office with this ugly man. All the other leaders agreed that the office of the software leader and the mechanical leader should be very close. As a result they had to stay together. *He is not only bad looking, he has a bad character too*, thought.

There was a retractable wall between their offices, but

Heff insisted that it be often open. As Apoll stepped into the shared office Heff said, "your work is late. You have to admit it."

Even his voice is so harsh, Apoll thought to himself. Noting Heff's criticism Apoll said, "I am content that everything is on schedule Heff."

Heff moved his fat and deformed body toward Apoll.

"I need to coordinate the sealing of the star gate tomorrow, and I'm not convinced you'll be ready with all the necessary electronics in place and tested." He smiled sarcastically at Apoll.

"As I said, all is on schedule," Apoll insisted.

"Okay …" Heff said in a low voice, unconvinced, "you know," he paused with a knowing look at Apoll, "that as leaders we are trained in everything …"

"And?"

"And, I know what are you are working on."

"And?" Apoll gazed at Heff with his beautiful face.

"Don't be ridiculous! You haven't installed the tracking device yet."

"I don't know what you are talking about Heff," this time Apoll appeared confused. He made a huge mental effort to control the muscles of his face.

"You can speak freely; I overrode the surveillance system in this room. You are not the only one who can do it." Heff tried to smile reassuringly at Apoll, but his smile was just a grin.

For a moment, Apoll was unsure how much Heff knew.

"Let's be practical, what exactly do you want, Heff?"

"I want to know what they're going to send through these star gates once they're operational."

PATRICK VAITUS

"But there's no secret …"

Apoll wasn't able to finish his sentence as he was rudely interrupted by Heff.

"Install that fucking tracking device quickly and let me start sealing the enclosure!" Heff roared to Apoll. But Apoll was not impressed at all.

"Why do you need to know what they'll be sending through the star gates?" Apoll smiled at Heff.

Heff attempted to back at Apoll and said, "Because I am a curious person."

Apoll took a moment to think intensely and run some possible scenarios.

"I'm not going to install any supplementary device Heff. I just realized it might pose a threat to the normal functionality of the star gate, and I don't want to take any risks."

"Then tell me what you think might go wrong, and let's fix it together." Heff grinned at Apoll again. He stepped very close to Apoll as though trying to intimidate him. Instead, Apoll appeared confident. He smiled politely at Heff:

"Let's do it together then, I am a curious person too."

"The atomic distribution of your DNA is still intriguing to me," Prom said. "It is out of the classical pattern."

"And why is that?" Arr asked.

"It cannot explain your bisexual behaviours," Prom answered sharply.

"I think you are mistaking me with Apoll," Arr said, with a critical smile at Prom.

Prom walked around the examination table where Arr

lay naked. Arr appeared to enjoy this. He had always thought his body was beautiful. Even more beautiful than Apoll's. His skin was just a little darker, but this color accentuated the harmony of his beautifully muscled body. His hair was black and curly. He discreetly watched Prom with his dark eyes.

Prom made a huge effort to appear undisturbed by Arr's nudity. He was wore a medical uniform that fit absolutely tight to his body. His body was also quite muscular, but as he was very tall, his body was still well-proportioned. His hair was long, black and straight. His green eyes were an important tool he used in the many seductions he had been involved in.

With a critical air, Arr asked, "are you sure you're mentally accessing my folder now and not Apoll's?"

Ignoring Arr's criticism, Prom continued to walk around the table, focusing deeply on his examination of Arr's nude body. The scanners sent him all the test results mentally through the computers. He knew by now everything there was to know about every molecule in Arr's body, and every detail with regard to his metabolism.

Finally, in a professional tone he answered Arr, "not at all. Apoll has a mind oriented towards the arts, music, and so on. I would expect some bisexual behaviour at least, if not a gay-oriented individual. But you, you are a violent character. I'm still working to find a correlation between your DNA's structure and your personality."

"And are you trying to find this correlation for your own curiosity, or has someone else asked you to do it?"

Again Prom ignored Arr's sarcasm.

"I do it for your benefit, not because Dem and Hest asked. I think that's what you mean by 'someone' else?"

Arr became serious. "Do you think they're watching us right now?"

"I would say no. However, they can read everything in the transcripts later. If there was any urgency, their computers would alert them mentally. You are a very important member of the crew, but I don't think you are an 'urgency' right now," and Prom smiled professionally to Arr.

"Do you think they can read our minds?"

"Unfortunately, they can … to an extent. But it is strictly forbidden without valid security reasons."

"I think they're doing it one way or another," Arr said adding a shade of sadness to his expression.

"I think you're wrong. Hest and Dem are highly ethical."

"Yes. Ethical to a point," Arr smiled bitterly at Prom. "A shifting point."

"What do you mean?" Prom became very serious.

"The current law allows them to play with the DNA from the data base in a very limited way," Arr started laughing, "combining only a certain ovule with a certain spermatozoid."

"They can make clones if the expedition requests it."

"Clones?" Arr smiled sarcastically at Prom. "I'm talking about human evolution. How can there be evolution if …"

Agitated, Prom interrupted him, "by an extraordinary mathematical analysis of all the possible DNA combinations from the two parents."

Arr started to laugh, "There can be many 'parents' as you call them. All they have to do is take the correct sequences from the correct DNA and make the correct combinations."

And Arr stood up, gazing at Prom, "there's no need to fertilize real cells. It is quite elementary."

"I know the process very well. But it is illegal. And if there's anything wrong with the newly-created being, we could be in danger."

Prom paused, gazing at Arr, "sorry, but I don't expect you to understand. You are a highly unethical person."

"Maybe that's why I am the war strategist, as opposed to the paltry roles that every one of the rest of you have on this mission," Arr replied with a wide smile.

"This isn't a fighting mission, so there will be no need to fight with anyone," Prom said, convinced.

"It doesn't matter; I still have to consider the possibility of our defeat at any moment." Arr said in a high voice, feeling nervous for a moment.

"Defeat? To whom?"

"Each other!" Arr was almost screaming now.

"Oh Arr, has your new student Afronda made you nervous?"

"In our database, there is clear evidence that she has psychic abilities, including precognition." Arr countered.

"Still, this whole story is based on a premonition." Prom was dismissive.

"I think you should study her closely, to find a relationship between her DNA, her premonition abilities and to advise Dem and Hest not to be so ignorant to the danger."

"Maybe the right person to inform is Zeu. There's nothing too much to do on this long hyper-flight, and I'm convinced everyone is watching everyone else." Prom paused and smiled convincingly at Arr. "So, how is your new student anyway?"

"As you said, everyone is watching everyone. I'm sure that you've watched her training records."

"Yes. But I was curious to hear your thoughts."

Prom appeared genuinely curious, which made Arr feel important again.

"Afronda is a wonderful student, except sometimes she is very tired after Atena 's meetings."

"Her body has developed more muscle mass. I am sure she finds it quite … unattractive for a woman."

"She doesn't care. And I admire her for it."

"Okay then. We'd better prepare for the next meeting."

"I know. All the main leaders are invited. Herm is quite finished his hyperspace jumps.

The people in cryogenic hibernation will wake up soon, and Zeu wants to say few things to us before then.

⸻ ◆ ⸻

Zeu, Herr and Herm were in the meeting room. They joked and laughed loudly. Herr and Zeu were dressed in white robes, which were well-fitted to their bodies. Zeu's attire was mostly open on his chest, to show off his chest muscles. Herr's dress was modestly cut to cover her breasts, but nicely accentuated the shape of her lovely body. Herm was dressed in a white suit fitted very tight to his body.

Soon, Apoll and Heff joined the others in the meeting room. Apoll was dressed in a white robe almost identical to Zeu's. Heff was dressed in a kind of working suit quite loose on his body which appeared to be somewhat dirty. Although Herr was sympathetic to him, she could not stop herself from thinking he chose to wear that kind of clothing to hide his deformed body.

Arr and Prom entered the meeting room. Arr wore black clothes that made him look like an old warrior. Prom was in a white suit with a hint of blue, worn somewhat tight to his body.

Taking an arrogant air, Arr addressed Heff: "I thought this was a seniors' meeting; we should show respect in the way we are dressed."

Suddenly, Zeu, Herr and Herm stopped laughing and directed their eyes to Heff. Unimpressed, as the all eyes in the room were watching him, Heff simply said, "I just transferred the last star gate device to Discordia. She will place it in space soon. I didn't have time for minor considerations like paying attention to how I was dressed for this meeting."

Trying to make peace in the room, Herr added, "At least make sure, in these kind of situations, that your collar is not dirty."

Zeu tried to end the discussion in a loud voice. "If Afronda is disturbed by the way you are dressed, you will have to go and change your clothes immediately. And I will accept no comments from your side Heff."

For a moment there was silence in the room. Arr was satisfied and smiled at Heff. Heff was ready to argue but stopped himself, as Afronda and Atena entered in the room.

A general inaudible *ohh* was flowing through the room. The two women were usually impeccably dressed and arrayed for any little festivity or leader's meeting, but now both of them were dressed in white fighting suits and were sweating profusely.

"So sorry," Afronda said, attempting to smile, "we didn't have enough time to shower or change."

They took the last two free chairs at the table.

Zeu looked around and counted the people in the room. Finally he said, "As all the leaders are present, I declare this meeting open."

"One moment," Aetna interrupted, "I don't see Discordia."

"I didn't invite her," Zeu said in a firm voice. "She is a sub-lead. This is a leaders' meeting."

The people in the room exchanged quick looks as though asking themselves *is that true*?

Understanding their looks, Zeu explained, "she is the leader of the operations team. But she and her team are subordinates to each one of you. Right now she reports to Herm. As Herm is here, I see no reason to invite her too. Herm will pass along the summary of this meeting or, she can watch it herself once the record is placed online. However, confidential content like this discussion about her will remain secret."

Zeu paused to be sure everyone in the room was in agreement.

"As I said," Zeu continued, "I declare this meeting open. This is my last meeting as your supreme leader. Very soon now, before the final hyperspace jump, our current supreme leader Uran will be woken from cryo-hibernation along with the other leaders Gee, Poss, Cronn and some general team members. I would like to take this opportunity to thank you all for your valuable help over the hyperspace flight. Mainly Herm, who coordinated the hyperspace jumps. Well done, Herm. And to Apoll for putting together the software of the star gate devices, along with Heff for completing the final closure of the star gate devices. Once we reach the planet Terr 271, our final destination, we will be able to communicate instantly through the star gate system, and to send and receive material items, technical equipment and last but not least, living beings."

Proud of what he had said he paused again.

Near him, Herr looked around the room positively, as if to say *it's true. We all did an awesome job.*

Suddenly their contemplative moment was interrupted as Discordia's holographic image appeared abruptly in the middle of the table. Her voice, although always thin and sharp, seemed even more thin and sharp now.

"*Priority zero,*" she said in a very loud voice. She swayed her tall and slim body as she just moved from her operator's displays.

"I hate when she does that," Afronda said in a low voice to Atena.

For a moment Atena looked at Afronda, then she looked back to the middle of the table where Discordia's holographic image was waiting for one of them to realize the importance of her words: *priority zero.*

"What is the emergency Discordia?" Zeu demanded in a calm voice.

"Sir," she said, "we have just discovered a malfunction in the star gate system. There appear to have been explosions in several of the star gates."

"Oh …" Zeu tried to remain calm, "Apoll and his team will immediately begin an investigation. Thank you for your intervention Discordia." As though her main task was now to contradict Zeu, Discordia continued:

"I have already done it, sir. Apoll can double-check, but you have to face the truth. We are isolated and cannot send or receive matter through star gates. We cannot even communicate. We are now completely isolated."

A cold silence descended on the room.

In a low voice Atena asked Afronda, "Is this what your premonition was about?"

Afronda looked absently at a blank wall and, without looking back at Atena said, "no. My premonition is worse than this."

CHAPTER 2

The threshold destination

*We didn't reach yet this planet
and... I know it has three ghosts.*

Afronda's secret journal

Afronda hates the cryogenic fluid. She believes it is disgusting, bad smelling, and its gel aspect makes her think of some disgusting expectorant of organic bodies. She also finds it almost incompatible with the skin's cells chemistry, despite the fact it was claimed to be compatible. She did a lot of work to prove its incompatibility. But given the current stage of technology it was a fact that this fluid is the only one capable to keep the human body well humidified during the cryogenic process. Also it was able to keep the human body remarkable connected with the electronic interfaces. Therefore, no one paid close attention to Afronda's warnings. She and her team worked a lot on this research, but no one accorded them the right attention. With a little consolation Afronda told to her team: "*in order to avoid this long contact of the cryo gel with their skin, the people should refuse the hibernation. The extending life components contained on our food work absolutely perfectly and without side effects. If one would choose hibernation with this disgusting hibernation fluid in contact with their skin, it is entirely their choice."*

Another example she gave to her team was that only four key leaders of this expedition have chosen the cryogenic sleep.

"But they are the supreme leaders of this expedition", Tetti a wonderful young lady, member of Afronda's team observed in a meeting. For a moment it was silence in the room. All the wonderful people members of Afronda's team turned their eyes to Tetti. Some of them turn their perfect bodies toward Tetti analyzing her better for this intervention. Afronda understood they hate Tetti in this moment because she dared to argue with her, their beloved leader. Afronda tried to quickly end this little conflict. *"Thank you Tetti. I have found this strange too. For this reason I asked Atena to investigate. I will have an answer for you, soon. "* The eyes of the people in the room moved between Afronda and Tetti. Tetti was smiling nicely to Afronda.

"Thanks boss. It is probably nothing. Please, pardon my intervention. "

"No problem Tetti. We are a team. We need to love each other."
And now, without care about the stupid cryogenic gel, Afronda was holding the hand of her beloved friend Gee. Afronda used all the mental training she knew to disguise her disgust about the cryogenic gel. All she intended to show to those who are now present in the cryo zone, and to the others watching trough spy cameras, was her love to Gee. And it was not hard for her. Afronda was a master

in face and mental dissimulate. But now, she had nothing to hide. She was really happy again with her loved friend Gee. Afronda felt safer near Gee. Gee's fighting skills and leadership skills was the absolute reason. Afronda felt much safer now. She started to think all her premonitions were nothing. *"And how stupid she was to share it with others. .."*

"Gee, are you OK?" Afronda asked with a voice that showed her concern.

Near them absolutely naked Uran the supreme leader of the expedition was seating with his eyes closed. Through his brain's chip he was scanning the data from all computers. Discretely Afronda was studying his face. She knew by now, none of the people from this ship are able to hide their human feelings. And she was extremely good in reading their faces. Any little face muscle contraction gave her indications of what they were thinking. *"I know if they are happy or sad, nice surprised or bed surprised. I know if they have a feeling, and what feeling. I know if they try to hide that feeling."*

Right now Afronda was a little bit confused about Uran. *"But he is a master in dissimulation too."* Also, near them Cronn, Uran's deputy. He was updating his data too. But Afronda was easily able to read his surprise with regard to the recent events. The loss of the star gates was a terrible issue, and it left the mission under awful consequences.

Close to their place Zeu and Herr were talking with Poss in a lower voice. They were happy to see their friend Poss woken up from cryo hibernation. Their faces didn't show too much emotions as they proved an exceptional face mimic control.

"Oh Afronda, Gee said in a low voice, I definitely need a very long shower. ...

But abruptly she stopped her talking as Uran stared boldly in their direction.

"A very short one should be enough", He said angrily.

In a male defensive voice Gee answered back " I know grave incidents has occurred. We need at least a few more hours to investigate. You can go on with your first general meeting when we are ready. Should I remind you that I am your deputy too?"

Afronda never saw Gee speak so aggressively to Uran. She was a little bit embarrassed to be there and to assist at this scene. For this reason she corrected immediately her facial expression to show this.

Emphasizing his words Uran said "I need all of you to be in the main meeting room in exactly one hour".

"But...." Gee tried again to talk.

She was rudely interrupted by Uran.

"Dem and Hest required this meeting to be run as soon as possible. Their perception about recent events is quite... tragically."

Gee answered in a calm voice "do not worry dear I will be ready, and you will have all my support."

The meeting room was full. Uran was looking to the people on his left and right. He sits on the chair of head of the table. He was dressed in a white robe quite large on his body but generously open at chest showing off his over developed muscles. He felt an impulse to touch his curly black hair but he resisted thinking it might appear as a wackiness gesture. On his right was sitting Gee and on his left Cronn. Both of them wearing the same white robes. Afronda was setting near Gee and she was touching Gee's hand. All the other leaders were wearing white dresses waiting in silence on their seats. At the other end of the table were two empty chairs. Athena was trying a visualization, thinking how Dem and Hest will sit there soon and how mad their faces will look like.

"All right," Uran said gazing all with a very critical look.

"We have only a few minutes until Dem and Hest will arrive. Let's have a quick discussion."

Like forgetting how precious time is until Dem and Hest's arrival he fixed his eyes on

Apoll and said nothing, only using this as an intimidation technique.

Trying to somehow save this moment Gee said "Arr is missing."

"I am sure we can start without him," Cronn said in Uran's place.

Uran continued to fix his gaze on Apoll, and finally he said to him in a heavy voice, "You are in a lot of troubles Apoll. You are the main one responsible for this situation and the report you prepared is totally unsatisfactory."

Apoll was very embarrassed to be criticized like this in the front of the all main leaders. All the eyes in the room were gazing him. Apparently he had no idea how he can build an efficient defense, and a cold silence took place in the room.

Suddenly, Heff's voice broke the silence.

"Uran maybe Apoll didn't mention in his report that

I was very late with my mechanical jobs and that was causing. ..."

"He mentioned it!" Uran screamed.

The people in the room were very started by his scream. Heff continued in a normal voice.

"I would like to work with Apoll to redo the report. We will go over all the records. If you agree to this, you will have a satisfactory report, soon."

Adding her contribution to save this difficult moment Atena said, "I can work with Discordia to make sure her operation team made no mistakes on launching the gate devices."

Stepping in the discussion Herr said: "Apoll, are you sure the computers or other very clever robots didn't try to do… something, just to take control on us ?"

For a moment a cold silence took place in the room.

Breaking it and trying to help Herr, Zeu said: "This is an important hypotheses that we have to carefully investigate. We need to be absolutely sure this didn't happen or won't happen."

Trying to use a normal voice Apoll said: "This is without a doubt. There is the critical logical loop of decisions where are involved the brains..."

He was unable to finish his sentence as Zeu screamed almost as Uran did before,

"I didn't ask you about those dammed brains. I am questioning if they are trying a strike."

Completing Zeu's idea Gee said, "They are the very motivated to isolate us in this point of space and time."

It was clear this hypothesis made Uran more nervous and he was unable to control his anger.

As a deputy, Gee concluded in a grave voice.

"Yes. We have to re check and re investigate everything. There is a reason for star gates' explosions, and we have to find it."

"Undoubtedly" Cronn completed her. He moved his eyes to Uran .

"Uran, please...all is a matter of time. We will find the failure. I...."

But he was not able to continue because Dem and Hest showed in the room followed by Arr.

The atmosphere in the room appeared to be frozen by now.

Discordia was waving her tall body to the holographic projection in the front of her two operators. The holographic projection was showing the record of the of the last star gate device that recently exploded and generated the chain explosions. Emm the fat young guy said to her without moving his eyes from the holographic projection, "We watched this 100 times by now Ma'am. Unfortunately we cannot find the failure." Turning toward the holographic projection and checking for a favorable angle, the dark skin operator John said, "the computers analyzed this a million times by now, and also no failure was found."

Without saying anything Discordia started laughing with her tiny laugh.

The two guys turned to her very curious to know why she was laughing.

Enjoying her laughing moments Discordia finally said,

"Computers? Did you say computers? I want you to carefully investigate whether the computers deliberately did it."

"How?" Emm asked.

"And for what reason?" John asked.

"They want to isolate us here." Discordia said emphasizing the words with her tiny voice. And enigmatic she turned her back to the two guys who were staring each other. Going to her cubicle Discordia started to study a complicated holographic projection with a lot of numbers.

After few moments counting the new terrifying hypothesis the two operators turned off the explosion movie hologram and open the projection of the logical loop control records. From outside of her cubicle Discordia appeared to focusing on the holographic projection, in reality she started a telepathic conversation.

"Dear brain number seven, I thought you sleep."

"I never sleep."

"You do. In fact you are as human as I am."

"However, I sleep very short time."

"Report me if the first two main brains are confident that there is not a computers' strike."

"They will recheck this. As soon as they will have a conclusion, I will let you know."

"The leaders are in a meeting and restricted my audiovisual access there… again."

Increasing her tonality on the telepathic conversation Discordia said, "Should ask you *expressly* in any situation like this to present me the summary?"

"Sorry Discordia."

"Please don't forget starting with now," she paused, "and remember, I said: please."

"Yes Discordia."

"Report to me, the brains three and four are confident that the ship is in good working parameters?"

"No doubt Discordia."

"Ask brains five and six, to confirm that we are at the right point of destination."

"Yes. They confirmed."

"And you dear brain number seven, what do you think?"

"I think we are at the right destination too."

"You don't find it strange?"

"I am not sure what exactly you are referring at Discordia."

"If the metal blinds are removed from windows, I can see the planet with naked eye. And, until now nobody was looking at that beauty."

"You are correct Discordia."

"Let's do it, you and me."

"Yes, looking to a beauty. You and me. As two lovers."

"Do not be stupid dear brain number seven. Love is a stupid feeling."

"Oh..."

"Instead, we can be good friends."

Discordia paused for a little while, after that she continued.

"As a good friend, I expect your complete report."

"Yes!?"

"Using your telepathic abilities you have to penetrate

leader's minds and to tell me who is suspected for this situation."

"Yes Discordia. I will."

Discordia smiled largely.

"And now let's have a look at this beauty my dear friend."

———◆———

Dem and Hest stepped in the meeting room. Their faces where like steal made. The atmosphere in the room was full of tension. All the leaders tried perfectly to control their gestures. They didn't want to upset the two ladies in any way. Arr was coming in with Dem and Hest, but after the two ladies took their seats he remained at their back with his muscled arms crossed on his chest. We was wearing a black collar tight to his body. Dem end Hest were dressed in white and very fashion dresses. Atena was quickly thinking that Dem and Hest were looking steal faces as in her mental projection. Afronda concluded in her mind that's one of the reason the owner choose these two ladies to administrate the mission. Their control was so perfect.

Avoiding any eye contact with any person from the room Dem said, "Why do we have to attend this meeting?"

Herm was blinking from his eyes. For a moment he was confused by Dem's question. In fact she asked him to arrange this meeting.

With a calm voice like imploring for peace Uran said, "Dem I understand the irony of your question. Because of the emergency of the situation you are forced to run this meeting. I deeply regret what has happened. Apoll presented me a report and I just told him that the report is unsatisfactory. ..."

As not comprehending what Uran was talking about, Dem and Hest were looking to each other. These gestures made him to become silent.

With a metal voice Dem said,

"May I remind you, our job is to make sure you are doing yours?"

In a peaceful voice Gee said, "All of us know our duty and we know your responsibilities are huge compared to ours. ..."

She was not able to finish all she intended to say as Hest was booming with her wrist in the table.

"Speak only when you are allowed woman."

A cold silence was penetrating the room. The word *woman* addressed to Gee was shocking all of them. Their faces were showing for moment their emotions. Gee let down her face. Her intention was to calm the two ladies by any available technique.

"You asked for a report?" Dem said. "I thought the interface was adjusted to update you for incidents like this in a regular basis when you are cryo hibernating module."

Uran had no time to answer as Hest said, "No Dem. He preferred to peacefully sleep. I told you he is not suitable for the supreme leader position."

Almost every leader felt that it would be better not to be in the room right now.

"Ladies please be reasonable. Give me a chance to prove you that I am able to handle this emergency."

These words had an acceptable good impact on them, and after a short pause Dem started to speak again.

"What exactly are you... investigating?"

Using a convincing voice Uran said, "I will coordinate a detailed investigation to find the failure. Also we estimated the artificial intelligence might be responsible..."

"Do you think we are stupid?" Dem interrupted him.

"I... I'm sorry?" This time Uran blinked his eyes in an surprising gesture.

For a moment Herr smiled in amusement. To find such a big muscle guy who considered himself an absolutely supreme leader dominated by two ladies.

Trying again to control the situation Uran said

"Ladies what else do you want me to investigate? What else can be..."

"Sabotage!" Hest screamed.

"W...what?" Uran was totally took by surprise.

A moment of general confusion, surprise, and fear was flooded in the room. There was even some murmurs.

Cronn stood up, "I cannot admit this..."

"Sit down!" Dem said to him in a imperative male metal voice.

"Do this one more time and you are a dead man." Hest was grinning at him.

Realizing the presence of the other leaders, Dem said, "all of you are under the effect of the martial law. Arr will give you a few more details. Now get out of this room. Only the supreme commander and the two deputies will remain."

The people in the room were exchanging wondering looks and murmuring.

"Dem, Hest" Atena said, "I would like to offer you my entire support in investigating this matter. My team is overqualified to handle this kind of situation. Please, let me to help you."

"I don't have time for explanations now Atena. I know your abilities but Hest and I will handle this matter." Dem even didn't look to Athena.

"But. ..." Atena was trying a new justification.

She had no time as Hest was almost screaming at her, "you are suspected of sabotage too Atena. We cannot let you run the interrogations under these circumstances."

"Now out. All of you!"

All the leaders prepared to left the room, except Herr.

With her eyes, Zeu was like imploring her to not dare feud with the two ladies.

"With all my respect for you ladies. I would like to stay in the room."

"No!" Hest said in an imperative voice.

"The other leader were stoned, and wondering about Herr's courage."

"This command is addressing to you too Herr."

"But compared to other leaders, I expressed my wish to remain. You should consider my request, even in this kind of situation."

Hest was prepared to scream again but Dem started to speak in an unbelievable low calm voice.

"Herr, I am sure you have no such stomach for what is going on in this room."

Enjoying the victory expressed by Dem's pleasing voice, Herr smiled to Dem. And she said almost with the same tonality and infection, "as you wish Dem. However, when I have the opportunity, I will prove to you that I have stomach for things even worse."

Saying this she moved her eyes to Gee addressing her a cold look. After that, all the leaders group walked out of the room in silence.

——◆——

In silence all the leaders stepped out of the meeting room.

They walked out to the garden and formed small groups.

"Sabotage. ..."

"Sabotage. .."

This was the subject of all little groups. They were speaking one to the other in low voices.

Near them Arr said nothing yet. He was enjoying his victory moment that he was by now the absolute leader. In a voice without any emotional inflections he said, "unfortunately all of you are under the martial low starting with now. You are going to be totally monitored by my team. You are not allowed to go outside of the ship for any kind of planetary investigation. .."

"Can you excuse us for a moment?" Herr interrupted him.

Feeling in charge Zeu started to talk.

"All of us have the duty to help Dem and Hest."

Instantly all the people stopped the talking. All the eyes were directed to Zeu. He didn't say to help the supreme leader Uran. Each lieder started instantly to make mental estimations.

Zeu never accepted Uran as the supreme leader, Herm was thinking.

He is a rebel in this matter, he desperately wants Uran's leader position, Prom said in his mind.

He is suspected by sabotage too, Atena estimated in her mind.

"In situations like this our supreme leaders are Dem and Hest. They can make any changes they want."

"They can make any changes that are better for us," Atena tried to complete, and she stepped closer to Zeu.

"No," simply Zeu said

For a moment a cold fear started to float in the garden.

"W... what do you mean?" Afronda asked in a shaking voice.

"He means, Dem and Hest have to do what is necessary for the paramount of the ship. As someone tried to sabotage the ship who knows what their secret protocol is, if they cannot find the saboteur. We might be disposable and only the ship is important." Herr added.

"But the hypothesis that the artificial intelligence of the ship is trying to do something against us in not totally eliminated," Heff said moving his ugly body to the center of the group. "Apoll and I have to investigate it."

"Good luck with this," Zeu said. "If you are not successful, and this is the most probable situation, we have to figure out who the saboteur is."

Herr was stepping closer to Zeu, "and this before Dem and Hest start to apply their *secret protocol.*" She was accentuating the last two words. Afronda tried to make up her mind *what a nightmare. ... still something is wrong. My premonition feeling was based on my own safety not group's safety. And... I cannot base my projection on a premonition....*

"So,..." Herr said, "who sabotaged the mission?"

"Who wants to see us isolated here?" Atena asked.

"The artificial intelligence. Even the brains of logical control loops. They might have wanted to test how we react in isolated condition." Poss said convinced.

"I agree this is a possibility." Zeu said. "You and Apoll have to investigate it."

"But still the main thing is to figure out if there was a sabotage act." Zeu paused and he was looking around the group. After a large breath he continued: "a human sabotage act".

The silence was flooding in the room.

"Okay! As requested, I gave you a moment to talk," Arr said gazing at Herr, "and that moment is gone."

Two muscular ladies heavy armed materialized in Arr's behind.

For a moment Apoll was thinking about the convenience of using the teleportation system. *These two ladies were materialized by teleportation. How useful was it if the star gate was in operation now. Any matter from our original planets was going to be sent here as we initially planned.*

"They are my assistants Hanna and Hanka and they will help me to..." but Arr was not able to finish his sentence as Herr interrupted him.

"Oh ... spare us." Herr said to him in a male voice.

--------◆--------

The tension was still floating in the meeting room.

"I hope at least you don't suspect sabotage from the deputy team lead by Zeu. He is very loyal. I am sure that if I was going to be in the same situation ..." He was not able to finish his sentence as Dem interrupted him on a heavy voice, "All of you are suspect!"

"Do not estimate our potential Uran," Hest added. Her face was almost saying now: *if you do it, you are already dead.*

"I don't." Uran said simply. "I want to assure you that you have all my support. I know in an emergency like this you can operate any change you want. Please ladies, you know my potential. Please let me, and my team, help you. If there is a sabotage act, we will shortly figure out how and who did it."

For a moment Dem and Hest said nothing. Like taking advantage of this silence moment, Gee said "any help in this situation should be welcomed. Especially from qualified teams such as ours." But Gee's words were freezing in the air.

"Or quite disturbing," Hest said on an icy voice, "you might try cover your tracks."

"If we do this, it will be a good opportunity for you to catch us." Cronn tried to control the emotions from his voice.

Dem and Hest looked coldly at him.

Unexpected Gee stand up. She turned her back to the meeting table. With lazy steps she walked to one of room's wall. Instantly it becomes transparent, and shortly it started to show the image of the nearby planet.

Cronn, terrified was watching Dem and Hest. *Gee whom always had a lot of courage was risking her own life.*

Instead of reacting negatively, Dem and Hest were looking with interest to the outside planet's view.

For a moment there was silence in the meeting room. All of them were looking out to the planet.

With lazy gestures Gee turned her face to the meeting table and in a polite voice she addressed Dem and Hest.

"Ladies it might be an emergency situation. We might be isolated here. But we are at the end of our trip. Please, look out at this beauty. Out there we have everything we want. Water, oxygen, minerals, potentially organics ..."

Without waiting for an answer, Gee turned back to the immense glass wall where the image of the planet was waiting in silence.

Hypnotized by the image of the planet Dem and Hest walked near Gee. Apparently, they totally forget about the emergency situation that they have to handle.

Cronn was wandering, *I don't know what technique this is, but Gee is using it astoundingly . She get results, therefore she saved us.*

Dem and Hest were still hypnotized by the beauty of the planet.

"It is indeed a beauty!" Dem admitted.

Hest was also captured by the planet's mirage, and she said:

"It is so... blue…"

CHAPTER 3

The Blue Planet

*Power, power, power, more power.
This is what all our leaders are
looking for. Because of it, they can
break the law, friendships, alliances,
they can go to sabotage. That's
why Dem and I, have to watch them
so closely. How strange... I seek
power too.*

Hest, Internal thinking.

"Are we ready to launch the spy devices?" Discordia asked
her control room operators in her tiny voice. She was
sitting behind her two operators. The two operators were
in their chairs operating with their fingers the holographic
projection. Emm the fat guy turned to Discordia. He was
still in the chair, as the protocol didn't specify him to stand
up in these kind of conversations. From his chair he looked
up Discordia. She was extremely tall and extremely slim.

Her black dress was made by an very elastic material tighten to her body making her to appear taller and more slimmer.

"All is ready boss. We can launch the spy devices at any moment." A victory smile flourished on Discordia's face. She knew in this moment she was the most important person on the ship. No leader was allowed to come in the control room while the martial law was in place. It has been several days since they were practically locked in their apartments. The martial law ordered by Dem and Hest forbid them to meet in large groups. To show their protest the leaders decided to spend their time in their apartments. However, Discordia knew all of them are watching her right now. Launching the SDs or the spy devices was a very important activity. Discordia was so proud she is in charged to lead it. The second room operator, John, was turning to Discordia too. Discordia was looking down to him. She appears to enjoy checking his quite dark skin.

"All is settled up to your voice command my lady," he said in an admiring voice.

Discordia allowed herself a victory smile again. She felt so powerful in this moment. Making her voice more tiny and louder than before she commanded:

"Launch!" The two operators were still watching Discordia for few seconds as they knew this made her to feel more proud of herself. And, they wanted their boss to be always in a good mood. She moved her eyes to the holographic projection. The holographic projection showed thousands of little balls leaving the ship with an incredible speed. They were flying to the planet's direction. After the suspected sabotage act any SD was checked three times at least. They are very complex little machines. Their design included antigravity suspension, lasers to destroy the eventual objects that might collide and tones of detection sensors including high performed video cameras. Also, each SD was able to send radio waves back to the ship from out of space or from the planet. They were dotted with very powerful lithium accumulators and small solar panels to recharge the accumulators. The two control room operators commented in a courtesy voice about the abilities of these spy spheres. They were quite proud about the science enclosed in the little spy devices.

"I am familiar with the abilities of these devices." Simply Discordia answered.

The big holographic image of the planet was projected in the control room. Around it, little images, numbers, letters, symbols started to show up. They were the results of the instant information sent by the SDs to the central computer. The little images were appearing from time to time showing particular pictures from the planet. The two operators started to operate with their fingers around the hologram. Excited, they were commenting about some preliminary interpretation in a loud voice.

"Amazing..." John the black skinned guy commented.

"Isn't it?" Discordia said in a tiny loud voice. After that she come closer to the operators and as wanted nobody else to able to hear what she will tell to her two operators. She said in a law voice, "we might not be able to figure out who the saboteur is, but at list this planet will have no secrets for us."

The meeting was supposed to be top secret. But Afronda demanded Apoll give her secret access to view everything from her private room. She used all her power of seduction to coerce Apoll to do such an *illegal* act. It was quite difficult, but finally Apoll was corrupted to a commit to a sexual act. She started to think his gay side is quite well developed. For her own curiosity she decided to find a way to keep him under close observation. His sexual life interested her. *At least knowing his secrets is a way to manipulate him*, she thought. She was thinking already to ask Addon, a very handsome blonde member of her team, to start a relationship with Apoll too. *It will be beneficially for both of them*, she was thinking. Now she paid closed attention to the image projected on a little tiny screen in her bedroom. Apollo didn't allow her to make any record. The only way was to use her own brain for mnemonic registration. She hated these situations. '*Why do we have computers and mental link to them?*' She asked Apoll. "This is a highly secret conversation. I understand you want to see it. But we cannot risk having a record that can be easily located at a simply search."

"I can protect the folder by passwords," she has argued.

"Do not be a naive girl," Apoll said. "No records! If you do not agree, it means you wasted your sexual talents in vain."

Now Afronda was paying close attention to the scene she was able to see on her little screen. She was wondering how Uran, Gee and Cronn can be humiliated like this. They have been standing up there waiting for more than ten minutes by now. They were watching Dem and Hest having their *traditional* dinner. The three where standing up near the large dining table. They were allowed to wear only work collars. Opposite to them Dem and Hest were very fashionably dressed. Dem was in a black long dress that was quite tight to her upper body and large down. Hest had quite the same kind of dress but white color. They appeared to be more focussed on the food than the three people who were waiting by the table. The table was nicely arranged in the old tradition. In the middle of the table where seven candles that made a cozy light on the table.

"Dem, you did a perfect choice selecting this meat recipe." Hest said.

Dem largely smiled.

"And the wine you selected is just perfect."

"Ladies," Gee said, "are you sure the food is correctly balanced from proteins and lipids point of view? I would still prefer the jelly food. It is rightly calculated and made by the food computers."

"You are very correct Gee," Dem answered politely, "we prefer it too. But, sometimes Hest and I enjoy having our *traditional* dinner."

"We use the resources from our own farm."

"I guess you have an impressive farm," Gee said. She was quite happy to have this opening discussion as she was hopping to calm down the two ladies. She knew they are still extremely mad after the star gates lost.

"We have our own life support system, farm and..."

"And your own research," Uran interrupted Dem abruptly. Hest put down her knife and fork. She addressed Dem a look with full of meaning. It was like asking *'Dem why should I still be patient when this male makes me so mad?'* Dem bitterly smiled to Hest like telling her, *'just a little patience my dear.'* Like totally ignoring Uran, she addressed to Hest.

"I think we need more wine here."

Hest approved with a smile.

Immediately Uran's replica appears with a wine vessel and he refilled the wine glasses. After that he walked out in the nearby room.

His apparition increased the tension in the room. The message was quite clear. It was like Dem and Hest said to Uran *'you are our servant. Nothing more.'*

In silence the two ladies had a sip from the wine.

Finally Dem turned her face to Uran and she said in a very calm and polite voice.

"Our experiments are not your business. Instead, your experiments are our business. You were not able to rise up the huge amount of money requested for this experiment. Therefore, this makes you an employee."

"I know this very well," Uran said. And he paused giving Dem time to enjoy her little victory.

"May I suggest you be quiet especially in the position you are in right now?" Hest added.

"But if the owner of the ship was here, he would fully understood my actions and...."

"But he is here." Hest interrupted him. "Dem and I are his direct representatives. We are in charge and fully prepared to represent his interests here."

"Yes. Uran said almost increasing his voice. But we are facing an emergency situation, and I am afraid you are not showing enough understanding."

Cronn was quite theorized by the way discussion was going. He started even to ask if Uran is aware that the two ladies have the authority and power to kill him without hesitation.

"We approved the planet's exploration by the SDs. That

was a decision showing enough understanding, isn't it Uran? We almost have a complete report regarding planet's status. We suppose not to approve this action because the ship is under martial law as the author of the sabotage was not discovered yet." Dem said diplomatically.

"Thank you again for this ladies. I want this expedition to be returned to its normal status. I am the Supreme Leader and you should trust me. I beg you to let me coordinate all."

"If all goes well." Simply Hest argued to him.

With a large smile Dem said, "as long as you have no answers regarding who sabotaged the star gates devices, you appear to us powerless." Her face become bitter suddenly.

"I was in the cryo sleep at that time." Uran tried to defend himself.

"We got it." Dem answered back in a sharp voice. "But now, that you are awake, you cannot go on making excuses. I have had such confidence in you as the Supreme Leader of this experiment." Dem walked to Uran and in a friendly gesture she touched his shoulder.

"Now, I need your reassurance that my confidence was not misplaced."

"I… I was in cryogenic sleep. How can I be responsible for something that was happening during that time?" Uran appeared troubled.

Dem bitterly smiled at him. She turned her back with lazy gestures like saying "I am not convinced." Finally she went back to her chair.

Trying to temper the discussion Gee said, "are you suggesting Zeu and Herr are somehow involved in this sabotage?"

"All of you are suspects." Hest said in an imperative laud voice.

"It is ridiculous to suspect Zeu. You are persisting in this sabotage theory, when a malfunction or an artificial intelligence complot is equal highly probable." Uran said indignities.

"I thought we already said you can investigate these two possibilities. However…", Hest said having a little sip of wine, "if you won't have a satisfactory report regarding all the possibilities, we might replace you."

"W… what?" Uran could not believing what he heard.

"I mean all your team," Hest said and she was looking toward Gee and Cronn.

Dem nodded to them in a metal voice, "we have this authority."

"You better have a dam good report for us," Hest continued.

Gee tried to intervene in the discussion again.

"With such a suspicions among us, especially at this leaders level, we can simply go back to our origin planet."

"That won't happen." Dem said firmly. "Next stage is to stabilize the planet. Its moon is not at the right distance and it creates serious disturbance on the planets circle. This step can take billions of years. If the owner would like to verify our status, as long as he receive no signal from us, he might send a new spatial ship on this direction."

"As we live an eternity, we have the time and patience to wait." Hest approved Dem's statement.

"Perfect," Gee said, "We will proceed with the new stage: the stabilization of the planet."

"But the planet might have at list prokaryotes," Cronn said.

The two ladies were gazing him. His words were producing some irritation on the two ladies

"We will see this in the final report." Dem simply said.

"We are the forth kind civilization," Hest said.

In her bedroom, Quickly in her mind Afronda was rehearsing the civilization ranks. Civilization rank one that uses the resources of its own planet. Civilization two, which uses the resources from its star system. Rank three civilization, that uses resources from its own galaxy. And us, civilization rank four that uses the resources from other galaxies.

"We have accumulated enough knowledge and history to base our conclusions. Also, we know the status of this mission." Hest completed her sentence.

Uran was still not convinced.

"How about the nearby planet ?"

"Do not touch it." Hest screamed.

"We will have a team lead by Arr, to watch it." Dem simply said.

"By Arr..." Uran repeated. He was going to say "by that idiot?"

"We don't need to pay too much attention to that planet. It was going to be a good chance to have a binary planetary system if there was a developed civilization. Unfortunately, that planet isn't capable to sustain life for long time as this one."

"Yes Uran," Gee said, "The other planet is quite little and its magnetic field not powerful enough to deflect the star's radiation."

Uran was looking back to Hest and Dem, "okay then. To find the authors of the sabotage and to stabilize the planet, that's next. Did we agree on these two points?"

"We already did." Dem answered.

In silence the three leaders stepped out of the room. Quickly in her bedroom Afronda switched down the meeting's interception. This was her appointment with Apoll.

Remaining alone in the room, Dem and Hest continued their discussion.

A little sound signal also informed Dem and Hest that Afronda is now disconnected. A large smile was flourishing on their faces.

"If we are going to replace this leaders' team, I am going to miss our friend Gee."

"Me to."

"And…Discordia with her friend Brain Seven and their little tricks…"

"Or, Afronda and her questionable manipulations."

"Tricks within tricks."

"They are mistaking as with some beginners."

And Dem and Hest began laughing.

All the leaders where in the huge empty meeting room. This meeting was another exception to the martial law that was still in place. All of the leaders were dressed in white and large robes. It was like a respect to the very important subject they were going to debate. In this moment they didn't focus at all on impressing Dem and Hest who was monitoring them right now. Or Discordia, who was watching them from the control room together with her two operators. Discordia was so intensity focused on them as she even didn't blink. The leaders were circling around the huge planet's hologram.

Poss was even touching the hologram. He exclaimed, "this planet is so blue, so beautiful so much wishing to host life."

"Actually, right now it is a poison," abruptly Herr interrupted him.

Like disturbed Poss addressed a angry look to Herr.

Trying to make pace Gee said,

"Unfortunately, the planet is not habitable right now. Despite the emergency situation of losing star gate devices, martial law and so on we are authorized to make some welcomed adjustments for this beauty. And, I am very happy." Saying this Gee was touching Poss's shoulder. "You will have gorgeous beautiful oceans here Poss."

"All right", Uran said in a very loud and disturbing voice. All the leaders who where day dreaming around the hologram appear to have woken up.

Continuing in the same loud voice Uran said,

"Let's listen Herm. He prepared a summary report. After that I need your opinion to decide what's next regarding the planet and its stabilization." Scratching in a quick move his wonderful body, Herm smiled to all of them. He made a discreet sign with his hand and the huge hologram disappeared. Now the room appeared so huge and so empty.

Herm was walking in the middle of the room . The other leaders have come close to him.

"The equipment we sent down to the planet gave us precise data. We are able to precisely estimate the history of this planet. We are almost 9.9 billion years from Bing Bang. The report I sent out will give you exact numbers. This solar system was formed 0.9 billion year ago."

"Quite a young solar system", Atena interrupted him.

"Yes." Simply Herm answered. "This planet was formed together with its solar system mainly from the cosmic dust. However this planet is special. It is like our habitable planets from many points of view. Our initial estimations that it would be the perfect candidate for this experiment were correct. Particularly, I am referring to the planet's core. It is a very hot lava that is rotating and it is able to generate a protective magnetic field around the planet. That's why the lethal radiation are deflected by planet's magnetic field."

Herm paused as he was looking around the room. All the leaders where watching him with great interest.

"0.8 billion years ago something terrible was happening with this planet."

"The collision with a huge asteroid", Heff interrupted him.

"I'm afraid that object was quite huge to be called an… asteroid. It was a planet."

"Do not be ridiculous Herm," Heff protested.

"Let's call that 'item' Thea," Gee interrupted Heff who was ready to continue his arguing.

"Thank you Gee." Herm has smiled politely to Gee.

"Here," in his behind has appeared a new holograph projection "is the projection of Thea. As you see the computers estimated it as a huge sphere and its dimensions allows us to include it on the planet's class. All these estimations were based on the post effect that our SDs determined on the blue planet's surface." Saying this he addressed an ironical look to Heff.

The hologram presented many numbers showing detailed information about Thea.

"It is almost the size of nearby planet Marr", Arr said. "Actually Marr is able to host life too. I will watch it very careful." Arr said proudly.

"It won't be able to host life as this one Terr 271. Marr's magnetic field is not that powerful." Herm abruptly concluded.

"It was so nice for the intelligent life of this corner of the universe to have two habitable planets so close." Afronda said almost like dreaming.

"I'm afraid until the intelligent life forms will be developed here, Marr will be a desolate desert planet unable to sustain life." Herr said, and she smiled to Afronda. "So sorry dear. We live in a hostile universe."

Afronda didn't answer.

"Herm you might continue," Cronn encouraged Herm.

"Ok. As Thea was coming with a terrible speed, of course there was a disturbing collision. Because of the impact the liberated heat transformed the whole planet into liquid. There where planetary waves. Also a massive quality of dust was sent out to the space. It is very possible at that time Terr 271 was looking like nearby planet Satt with its rings. The planet's moon was formed from this dust. And here we are. With the moon around planet. However, the moon is quite close or too close to the planet. Please check the numbers on the hologram. Decades after moon's formation the planet cooled down. Right now the spin rotation of the planet is too high. As a result, currently planet's light days are around 3 hours longer and the entire day including the night it would be 6 hours in total.

"Oh.... we need to go over 20." Athena said.

"Maybe", this time Herm appeared not enjoying interruption. "This is an effect of the impact with Thea, or over spinning Terr."

"I wish this planet to change quickly in a positive way of evolution." Herr said coming closer to Zeu.

"We will accelerate the positive evolution. We have the necessary technology, " Uran said smiling at Herr.

"Unfortunately it will take millions of years," Cronn observed.

"We can wait. We have time." Afronda, said in a conclusive voice.

"This Is not a recreational mission. We are immoral, we have a mission here and we volunteered for this mission." Herr completed Afronda's idea.

"All right." Uran said. "How about the chemical composition? Do we have enough needed inorganics to promote life on this planet?"

"There are some good stuff. The chemical composition, here on the holographic projection, shows ...." but Herm was not able to finish his idea.

"Not enough Carbon and Nitrogen." Gee interrupted him impolitely.

"All right. Conclusions ." Uran demanded looking around the room.

"Planet's magnetic field is strong enough to deflect the solar radiation at an acceptable level. The planet will be able to sustain life." Apoll said.

"The moon is too close to the planet and it creates a major disturbance. We need to move it away at the right distance." Zeu said.

"The planet is spinning too fast. We need to decrease its spinning. We need more than 20 hours day and night together." Athena said.

"Not enough chemical elements for life." Herr said.

"Not enough water. I want more." Poss added.

"I want it more stable and beautiful…" Afronda added.

"Very well. We need to stabilize the planet. Dem and Hest approved these activities to be done in parallel with the investigations for star gates failures. Let's split the work then." Uran concluded. "Let's run some more precise calculations. Gee, calculate what needs to be the optimum distance between planet and its moon. Athena, what's the optimum rotation speed of the planet we want to reach… around 24 hours I will guess? Herr, what more for inorganics do we need on the planet? Kinds and quantities? Poss, how much water you would like to have here? How much to make you happy, I mean."

Uran paused a while and finally he was turning to Herm.

"Wonderful report Herm. Once these requested calculations are done, you and Discordia would like to play with some meteorites. Big meteorites. But …" Uran raised a finger, " no organics are allowed. We have enough troubles already. We don't need extra problems specially now when we are under the martial law."

CHAPTER 4

Stabilizing the planet

We are all attracted by visual appearances.

Poss, delivering teachings

Dem and Hest stepped in the room. They were very stylishly dressed. Hest was carrying a little square purse. The room appeared totally empty, except there were seven tall cylindrical vessels. They were totally transparent and inside them, floating in a light yellow liquid, were the necked brains. Each brain was in its own cylinder; seven brains in total. Little air bubbles appeared in the bottom of the vessels and traveled to the top. The brains were sitting quietly in their own vessels. At the bottom of each brain were tiny metal wire connections. They connected the brain with the ship's control systems. All the decisions of importance for humans had the control brains' decisions in their final loop. However, if there were decisions of paramount importance, even the brains could not make a final decision. At this upper level, the final decision belonged to the human beings, meaning control room operators, Discordia, the leaders or the supreme leaders. Each of the brains had its redundant correspondent, so if one was actively working in the decision loop, the other one was allowed to sleep. The first two brains were in charge of the computer's control, mainly the software part. Brains three and four were watching the hardware part of the computers and generally the mechanical integrity of the sheep. Brains five and six were working as UPS, or as leaders of the Universe Positioning System. They knew in detail each corner of the known universe and they were able to estimate precisely the position of the ship in every corner of every galaxy. They were able to precisely estimate the super light jumps of the ship. The last one, brain number seven (or the seventh brain), was incharge with mental activities like telepathic communication and reading humans' minds.

Each of them has an redundant pair, except brain number seven! Hest was thinking. She had already discussed the lab difficulties regarding the producing of a secondary brain with telepathic capabilities with Dem. *That's why this bastard doesn't have a redundant pair yet!* Hest couldn't stop thinking.

Despite the fact that the room was 'apparently' empty, it had a terrifying defensive system. Lasers were hidden in the walls, along with deadly chemicals and biological release weapons, and other devices. If an intruder penetrated the brains' room, he was suppressed totally and instantly. It didn't matter if the intruder was human or robot. Nobody had access to this room except Dem and Hest, not even the supreme leaders. At this very moment all the defensive systems were shut off at Dem and Hest's command.

Dem and Hest were walking toward to Brain Seven's container. They remained in front of it for several seconds without saying a word. The flow of air bubbles increased in the brain's container. It was a sign that the brain was scared and due to this emotion its oxygen demand had increased.

He is afraid of us. Good! Dem was quickly thinking.

The two ladies where looking around the room.

"Leave us." Dem commanded.

The cylinders with the six brains slowly slid down to the floor. Finally they disappeared totally.

Once the two ladies were alone with Brain Seven's container, Hest opened the little square purse with precise gestures. From there she took a syringe. For a moment she checked the syringe's needle and the green liquid contained in the syringe. It was easy to understand that green means poison, death.

With lazy gestures Hest came close to the brain's container. There was a little rubber piece. She was preparing to penetrate the rubber with the syringe needle and to inject the green liquid inside.

"What ... what is in the syringe?" the voice of Brain Seven could be heard trough speakers hidden in the walls.

"Poison," Hest answered simply.

"Please ... please ladies, let's talk first ..."

The level of oxygen bubbles increased dramatically in the container.

"There is nothing to talk about!" Hest said. "We simply don't need your services any longer."

"But this is not a reason to kill me. You can simply disconnect me."

"No!" Dem said. "You are particularly in the control brains series. Your telepathic abilities will still let you interact with the people. Unfortunately for you, death is the only way to stop you interacting." Dem's face was very grave.

"Particularly, interacting with Discordia," Hest added accentuating every word.

"Ladies, there in a mistake! You misinterpreted my interactions," The voice in the speakers sounded tragically.

With a precise gesture Hest screwed the container's little rubber piece with the syringe's sharp needle. Now the top of the needle was in the container's liquid. With only a push on the syringe's piston, the lethal poison would be inside the container. Instant death was near for Brain Seven.

"Please, please … all I told her was non-confidential information … nclassified information," his voice was shaking terribly.

"Even for this, you deserve to die," Hest answered with a voice of steel.

"But, I am sure I can find a way to make you thankful again. Please! Please …"

"How?" interrupted Dem. "Hest please wait," she said

Hest removed her hand from the syringe. Now the syringe remained suspended with its needle inside the container, penetrating the little rubber piece.

"But Dem, we already agreed …" Hest said in a confused voice.

Dem addressed Hest with a look that said, *let's give him a little chance.* Dem repeated her question abruptly: "How?"

"I can continue this game with Discordia and let you know all her thoughts."

"And how can be this in any way useful?" Hest smiled ironically, and with lazy gestures, moved her hand back to the syringe.

"She and her thoughts are not so insightful to us. Just a little piece on our complicated puzzle. We can monitor everything. Including your activity, as you see."

"I suspect she knows something about sabotage," Brain Seven's voice sounded normal coming from the wall speaker.

"What did you say?" Hest's hand stopped in the air midway to the syringe.

"I suspected she was involved in something, and that's way I started this game with her."

"Why you didn't inform us?" Dem wondered.

"I did. I made this observation in your private shared drive."

Dem and Hest simultaneously accessed Brain Seven's diaries. The information was indeed there.

"It is only a single sentence amongst a ton of information," Hest observed. "You should have emphasized its importance," she finished with an angry tone.

"You should have let us know if you were going to plan this strategy game. You should have labeled it as a strategy in your diaries," Dem said.

"This was a mistake, and I am ... so sorry. But, I was not sure how guilty she was. I am still not sure ..."

"This hypothesis needs to be carefully investigated," Dem said in a convinced voice." She shot a questioning look at Hest.

"Let's say we believe you ... at this time," Dem said in a

peaceful voice. "But in future, when you start a conversation with Discordia, you must inform us. We will monitor you more carefully from now on," she waited for a long pause, "if we let you live."

"I will," Brain Seven answered.

"We will reanalyze your electric waves and their intensity at the time you were in telepathic conversations with Discordia. We will know if you lie to us. If we find something suspicious, we will return," Dem concluded.

Hest removed the syringe with lazy gestures. She put it in the little purse

"One more thing," Hest added, "never do something that can be called a mistake."

Hest moved her head closer to the container and said in a very convincing voice:

"It might cost you your life!"

Discordia was waving her tall body. She was dressed in a long white robe made from a very elastic material. The robe was fitted very tightly to her body, which made her appear taller than she was in reality. The door in front of her automatically opened and she stepped into the room. The room was completely white. As the door closed behind her, Discordia had the sensation that she was in a white universe. There was no beginning and no end. Even her white dress was a part of this white universe.

They want to intimidate me. She was thinking quickly. In this moment, she tried to make every effort to prevent her mind being read. She started to think of memories from her childhood associated with the color white. The white sheets on her bed, the white room's wall, her white dresses, and so on. She was sure if she was activating and intensifying the *secondary thoughts* —as they were commonly called – then reading her mind would be nearly impossible. At this moment she trusted no one. Not even her friend, Brain Seven.

A few steps front of her, Arr materialized trough teleportation. He was wearing a black fighting costume. He was looking down. He lifted his head slowly to meet Discordia's eyes.

"If you think you are intimidating me, I have to advise you that you are wasting your time!" Discordia stated in a tiny, angry voice.

Proud of himself, Arr smiled back at Discordia. "The intention may appear intimidating, but the main propose of this meeting is the interrogation."

"Either way you are losing your time!" Discordia answered in a sharp voice.

"I advise you to be cooperative," Arr said in a normal voice. He made a huge effort to calm himself down. "You might know by now that patience is not one of my virtues. For somebody in your position, cooperation is the smart thing."

"Ask me questions then," Discordia said. "I am a busy person and you are abusing my free time."

"This might take a little while. You'd better forget about your busy schedule today."

"Why are you doing this to me?" Discordia deliberately emphasized each word.

"Discordia," Arr tried in a friendly tone, "I interrogated

all the team leaders like this ..." He paused in order to accentuate his next words, " ... and all of the supreme leaders."

Arr paused to allow the computers to search for any input in Discordia's mind or any facial interpretation.

Discordia was not able to stop a thought from forming, *Atena was much better for this job.*

"I interrogated all of them, including Atena." Arr said in a high voice.

This time Discordia managed to stop her thoughts by running through childhood memories in her mind. She was terrorized by how accurately her thoughts were read.

"Atena is suspected too, that's why she cannot conduct the interrogations. You have no reason to be frustrated, Discordia."

"All of us are suspected. But I would like to assure you, Dem and Hest, that I am completely innocent." Discordia said in a convincing voice.

"Seat down Discordia."

Arr said this and instantly two white chairs appeared from the floor.

With a polite gesture, Arr invited Discordia to take a seat.

"No thanks. I'll stand," Discordia answered quickly.

"As you wish." Arr said and he installed himself comfortably in a chair.

"Not sure how Atena was going to conduct this ... interview, " Now Arr appeared to be a little bit amused. "You already invited me to ask questions, but in fact, I am going to make two statements. Your comments on them will be greatly appreciated."

Discordia submitted by bowing her head. More, she decided, with lazy gestures, to sit down.

"First, I have gigantic admiration of your work and your capabilities. But I am not able to understand how you were not able to detect the possible malfunctions of the star gates devices before they were launched."

Discordia was blinked quickly.

"And second," Arr continued in a philosophical voice, "I'm not sure what are your real intentions were when you seduced the seventh brain."

Discordia smiled bitterly smiled at Arr.

"Am I to understand that as you didn't find the saboteur, you are trying to pin it all on me?"

"Not at all. As you are a very clever leader, perhaps you can convince me that you are not the saboteur."

"As I said, I am innocent."

Discordia paused and gazed Arr. Arr tried to smile nicely at Discordia.

"I interrogated all the leaders, and all of them said *I am innocent*. And yet, there was an act of sabotage," Arr said in a calm but convinced voice.

"Let's start with the second statement," Discordia said in a low voice. "That is a private relationship, and I would like to keep it private."

"But there was confidential information!"

"There was no confidential information," Discordia's voice rose. She paused to gaze at Arr.

"Arr, everything I did was in the interests of this mission. There was no breach of confidence. There is a personal matter. Surely you can understand this," Discordia smiled bitterly at him, "I was hoping the seventh brain could help me to find the saboteur and to give him to you, Dem and Hest."

"I appreciate it," Arr answered. "However the interrogation is going to take a little bit longer than was initially expected," he was ground the words out to Discordia.

Uran, Gee and Cronn where walking around a huge holographic projection. The other leaders were arriving in the room one by one. Once they stepped into the room, the first sensation they had was that the room's walls just disappeared, and that the huge hologram projection was the only thing in the entire universe.

A blue planet with a single moon. A moon too close to the planet. It was quite clear that the moon was causing disturbing gravitational effects on the planet's atmosphere. From time to time, meteorites passed close to the planet, some of them even hitting the planet or its moon. The hologram was very well projected as they were able to see this in very accurate detail.

"I want this planet to be more blue. I want more water there," Poss said once he stepped in the room, attracting everyone's attention for a short moment.

"You will have more water there," Uran said simply.

"This will be an easy task. There are many icy comets and meteorites around holding water within their crystal salts."

"Yes," Atena said walking around the hologram.

She and all the other leaders where dressed in long white robes. Usually when they had an important decision to make, this was their dress. It was like a symbol of democracy.

Just paying attention to this detail, it was easy to recognize the white meetings when the videos were replayed. Only Arr was dressed in a black tight collar. It made a discordant note compared to the others. It was like saying: *I am not on your side. You are still under martial law. I am the one who controls you. Dem and Hest empowered me to do it.*

"Having more water on the planet will be easy. All what we have to do is to disturb the orbit of these little comets and direct them to the planet," Atena continued.

"But make sure they contain no organics," Afronda observed. "Otherwise it will be in conflict with the objective of this experiment. The experiment's objective is to create intelligent life from inorganics at a planetary scale."

"Exactly," Cronn agreed. "The two first difficult task consists of moving the moon away to the correct distance and decreasing planet's rotational speed."

"This is going to take a large part of our resources," Prom observed.

"Yes," Uran said. "I guess all of you carefully reviewed the detailed plans made by Herm. The biggest meteorites will pass close to the moon and their gravitational pull will attract it away from the planet. Some of them will be directed to smash on the moon or will pass near the planet in the opposite rotational direction. This will slowly diminish the planet's rotation."

"How are you going to move such a large amount of meteorites?" Prom asked.

"Quite easily," Herm answered. "We will generate explosions on nearby meteorites. There will be atomic, antimatter explosions, and so on. I made detailed calculations. We will disturb the smallest meteors first, and they will modify the trajectory of the larger meteorites. Finally, we will use the biggest meteorites to correct the planet's rotation and to move the moon in the direction we want."

"As you can see," Uran completed Herm's statement, "in the end, the moon will be moved to the correct distance to balance the seasons on the planet as well. Also, the planet's rotation will be reduced to bring the total day of the planet to 24 hours. All of this will be done thanks to Herm's brilliant plan and at a reasonable energy consumption."

"Let's start then," Zeu added.

"There is a little problem," Gee said in a convinced voice.

"There is no problem," Herr said.

The two women feuded for a moment with their eyes.

"Time is the problem," Gee said. She looked around the room.

"This plan is brilliant, but it takes too much time," Cronn added.

"We have time!" Afronda said accenting each word. "We live an eternity. Time is not relevant to us."

"Well then … there will be some improvements of the plan. Discordia will start to execute the first steps immediately," Uran tried to make peace in the room.

"If there is nothing more, I shall adjourn the meeting."

"One more thing," a heavy voice sounded in the room. All eyes where on Arr.

"There will be no physical contact between any of our devices and the meteorites that will collide with the planet."

"And why is that?" Gee added in a bitter voice.

"I need to make sure no organics from our side are

artificially sent to the planet. This is the mandatory way of doing this. Dem and Hest instructed me to carefully watch the process."

Gee made an acceptance sign. "It is not a problem. Physical contact with the meteorites was never a technique involved in this plan."

"And," Arr tried to smile around the room, "do not forget you are under martial law. Do not send out anything until you have my approval. My team will carefully investigate everything."

"This will slow down the plan. It will take even more time," Gee said in a sad voice.

"We have time," Afronda said.

Gee shot her a not very peasant look.

Dem and Hest analyzed the holographic projections and the mathematical data for more than three hours. They were in their private projection room.

"It seems to be a good plan, " Dem said waving her body against the hologram.

"Yes indeed," Hest approved. "It will take a little bit longer than we estimated initially, but finally the planet will be well stabilized. The key is to ensure the moon is at the correct distance, and I am confident that Herm did the correct estimations."

"I agree," Dem said standing in a vertical position. "Related to our eternal lifespan, time is not important. They can indeed come up with a 24 hour total planet rotation, and this will be perfect."

"Still … I am not satisfied with the final estimated chemical composition."

"What do you mean?"

"Too much water. Poss has such influence on all leaders. It appears no one can refuse him. He asked for too much water. We should not approve the entire quantity …"

"Sorry to interrupt," a melodious computer voice sounded in the room. "Afronda is approaching."

What? She has no scheduled appointment with us!" The two ladies were very surprised.

"Is she armed?" Dem asked.

"Negative," the computer voice answered immediately.

"Scan her mind," Hest commanded abruptly.

"I have concluded she is quite peaceful," the computer voice answered back.

"Brain number seven?" Dem said in a interrogative voice.

"The telepathic waves of her brain are quite peaceful," the associated voice of Brain Seven sounded in the room.

Dem and Hest gazed at each other in silence for several seconds.

"She seduced Apoll and now she tried to manipulate us!" Hest concluded abruptly.

Dem smiled at her, "at least she is a very entertaining person … and we could use a break here."

One of the room's walls became transparent. Outside it, Afronda was walked with small steps, getting closer to the entrance door.

"Open the door," Dem commanded. She preferred to give the command to the computer by voice and not mentally. It was like she was trying to calm herself down.

Afronda stepped in the room. She smiled broadly to the two ladies and waved hello. She moved closer to the holographic projection.

"It seems to be a good plan. I am confident that with this chemical composition the intelligent beings ultimately produced will be … beautiful."

"We hope so. The program clearly states that you will be the one who will decide how they will ultimately look."

With a few lazy steps Afronda come closer to Dem and Hest. She smiled broadly at them again.

"Do not worry creatures, I come in peace," she murmured. Her face was very serious.

Dem and Hest burst out laughing with great pleasure. They laughed for around a minute. Afronda did the same.

When they calmed down Hest added, "my Dear, I would still like to advise you that we are not that easy to manipulate."

"At least, not as easy as Apoll." Dem added.

Afronda smiled again.

"You might think I am powerful, but I only do this because my life is in grave danger." Her voice was shaking, and her face became sad. A few tears appeared in her eyes.

"Oh dear! You are overreacting. It's all just your imagination," Dem tried to calm her down.

"I am sure it is not only imagination," said Afronda sadly.

Dem came closer to Afronda and carefully studied her wonderful face. So white. So perfect.

"What do you feel exactly? Share with us something that you didn't mention at Arr's interrogations."

"As I said it is an .... elusive premonition. But it warns me of grave danger. A threat to my life."

"If it is elusive, maybe it's nothing," Hest tried.

"My dear, nobody on this ship wants to hurt you in any way. We all love you," Dem said smiled widely at Afronda.

"We will do everything to protect you," Hest finished. For a moment, the room was silent. Afronda's eyes were red, as though she had been crying.

"Is this connected to something?" Dem pointed to the holographic projection where the blue planet ad its moon were waiting in silence.

"Is there a time line, or something that might help us to increase our vigilance at a particular moment?"

Afronda's face showed that she was deep in intense thought.

"Yes, it is." Afronda said. And she moved her eyes from Dem to Hest and back. After a long pause she continued, "it is connected with prokaryotes."

"Prokaryotes?" Dem and Hest said almost simultaneously.

"Yes," Afronda said simply. "Prokaryotes."

"Please, help me. Help me at that particular moment," Afronda implored them this time.

"We will dear. We love you."

"We truly love you. We will do everything to avoid any tragedy here."

Afronda smiled bitterly at them.

"Thanks a lot ladies," She embraced the two ladies and she left the room.

Dem and Hest were looking at the door where Afronda had just left.

"Oh Dem, I am so … tired."

"I am tired too."

They continued to watch the door.

"One way or another, we should finish this."

"Yes."

"That saboteur criminal covered his trucks so diabolically well!"

"Still, there is always hope."

"I don't know how, but Afronda is correct. We cannot risk the prokaryotes' timeline as long as the criminal -- or criminals -- is part of the current crew."

"Yes. We have to apply the SP, the secret protocol."

Hest walked over and stood close to Dem, "meaning we have to kill them."

Dem nodded, "yes. We have to kill … all of them."

CHAPTER 5

The inorganic planet

It is amazing how life can appear and survive in the most abiotic places.

Gee, journal notes

All the leaders where ready for the trip. It was the first trip with leaders within the planet's atmosphere. It was a very rare trip, as they were still under martial law – such a long and boring wait under the circumstances. All the leaders were very excited about the break. Afronda was the only one who refused the trip. She had said the records transmitted by the life cameras were enough for her, and she also blamed the fatigue that she had felt for several days. As if by a miracle, however, her fatigue disappeared unexplainably on the day the trip was scheduled. So now she found herself standing along with the rest of the leaders waiting to board the ship. All of them were wearing tight collars. It was a good opportunity to show their wonderful bodies almost in a naked way.

However, there were by now two exceptions. As usual, Heff looked horrible in a tight collar. His deformed body looked more disgusting than ever before. The second exception was Discordia. Her body was simply too tall and too slim. She appeared almost like an alien from another planet compared to the rest of the crew. She was very silent but totally focused on the attitude of the other members. *Who can be the saboteur?* She asked herself. Her thoughts were interrupted by Afronda's words.

"I was expecting a different kind of ship," Afronda said, "something much more … aerodynamic, because this planet has an atmosphere."

"No need for anything like that yet," Heff answered, "our circular ships are able to move perfectly in any kind of space and they are able to provide us with a comfortable level of gravity at a very low cost."

Still Afronda was unthankful.

"But, it looks like a plate. As the shape doesn't matter to you, I will generate a report to forbid this shape. We need beauty in everything," she concluded in a serious voice.

Herr smiled to Afronda in a nice way, "you should add some square plates to your kitchen, dear."

"Alright," Uran interrupted their little chat. "Are you ready for boarding? Athena, did you check everything?"

Athena nodded a *yes* to him.

"Are you totally satisfied? If you need more time we understand."

"Thanks. I am completely satisfied. Once we are on the ship there is no danger of transporting organics to the planet. The ship is completely sealed and disinfected. I am confident that no DNA will be transported to the planet via this trip."

"Very well then," Uran said, "why don't we go inside?"

One by one the leaders stepped into the ship. Discordia had to bend her tall body in order to enter the ship. They took their seats and the automatic belts created a mesh on their bodies as soon as they were seated.

"This little ship is totally automated," Herm said. "But I still prefer to manually control it." He smiled around at the others, "that way, I feel like I am touching the planet."

"All ready? Let's go." Uran commanded.

It took only several minutes for the little ship to navigate from the massive galactic travel vessel to the planet.

We are penetrating planet's atmosphere right now," Herm announced.

At that moment, the ship's walls became totally transparent and all the leaders gazed out. It was as though they were in a glass enclosure, able to see all around.

Gee stood up and addressed the other passengers, "as you can see, the planet is quite stable now. There are no major storms, and the ocean waves are not very large. This is the direct effect of our actions. We moved the planet's moon to the correct distance; now the planet is in perfect equilibrium with its moon. The moon's attraction is stabilizing planet's atmosphere."

"It is quite dark," Athena observed.

"Yes," Gee admitted simply. "Actually there's not much to see here right now anyway. It is just a dead, inorganic planet."

"However," Herr interrupted "I like the feeling of being within planet's atmosphere."

"Do not forget it is toxic right now," Gee shot a critical look at Herr. "You can see its chemical composition here in this hologram. The atmospheric composition detected instantly by the ship's sensors."

"If there's nothing too much to see here, let's go under water," Poss proposed.

"Yes," Gee approved. "We might have something to discuss there."

The ship banked sharply and dove beneath the water's surface.

"The air temperature at the surface is quite scorching, but as we descend toward the sea floor, the temperature reaches almost freezing," Heff added.

"This water is so dirty," Afronda spat, disgusted.

"It will be clean soon," Poss answered politely.

"Soon?" Gee asked in an ironic voice. "How many billions of years will it take?"

"A few," Poss answered politely. "I always thought you were patient."

"Why is the timing so important to you, Gee?" Afronda asked. "We are immortal. We have enough time to wait. All we need is a little patience."

"Many billions of years don't pass quickly to me," Gee shot back, a little bit upset.

"Actually, Afronda's point of view is good. We need to understand why the water is so dirty. And the answer is right there," Herr said in grave voice.

All the leaders looked in the direction indicated by Herr.

"It's like a factory under water. See those little volcanoes? That smoke is in fact very hot, and there are minerals coming from underground. This is how the water gets hotter and collects minerals. All around us are only inorganics. Please look at the chemical composition on the hologram." Herr paused for a while, giving time for all the leaders to take in the information.

Finally he continued in a deep voice, "you could say we are in the chemical soup that soon will create life on this planet."

⸻ ❖ ⸻

Dem and Hest stood around the hologram of a huge DNA molecule. The holographic projection made it look like a column that rose from the floor to the ceiling of the room.

"It is so …"

"Beautiful …"

The two ladies stood in silence again contemplating the holographic projection.

"It is like a symphony."

"It is perfection itself."

"I can't believe we did it, Hest."

"We did a good thing, stealing this mathematical model from our owner," Hest said very convincingly.

"Do you think he wants us to perform this experiment?" Dem asked without making eye contact with Hest. She was studiously checking the hologram at its atomic level; the detail of the structure almost seemed to hypnotize her.

"Irrelevant," Hest answered, sounding upset. "The possibility of sabotage was not totally eliminated. We are now completely isolated without any ability to communicate," she stood for a moment to observe the hologram. "We'd be stupid if we didn't go on with this secret experiment."

PATRICK VAITUS

Dem began to circle the hologram. "The health of this individual will be extremely robust due to its perfect immunity system," she observed. "His mind will be sharp and brilliant. The problem is: he will be smarter than us …"

"Yes …"

"Will we be able to control him?"

"Yes."

After a pause, the two women gazed at each other.

"We will implement and activate the electronic chip in his brain once he is born. We will then be able to read his mind, his emotions, his thoughts," Dem said in a reassuring tone.

"And if he doesn't obey us?" demanded Hest.

"That little electronic thing has an explosive device too," Dem reminded her. "If he disobeys us, his brain will explode inside his skull. It is not a pleasant death. He will have reason to fear us, as should all the members of this ship. We can make their brains explode by issuing a simple mental command."

"Still, I'm not convinced. Creating intelligent life from a mathematical model …"

"It is an extrapolation of what our DNA might become after eons of genetic mutations … a very long time, even on the universe's scale. I only worry about one little detail, though. When our computers are assembling the molecules, if anything should go wrong … it could be a terrible mistake …" Dem pondered the staggering complexity of the problem.

"That would represent a rather unsuccessful experiment, I should say," Hest argued.

"One little misalignment, if even one tiny atomic

combination goes awry, then … then we will have created something entirely different," mused Dem.

Hest became agitated. "If we see he is a different individual than what we were expecting, we will have to kill him without hesitation," she asserted.

"It would have to look like an accident."

"Why? Nobody is watching us," retorted Hest. "Quite the contrary; we see everyone and everything."

Dem prodded her, "and the records?"

"We will delete the records."

Again the two ladies were silent.

"You know … he is not yet even created and yet when I look at this molecule, I have the distinct sensation that he's watching us," whispered Dem.

Hest shuddered. "How strange, I feel the same."

CHAPTER 6

The organic planet

Some universes exist only in our minds.

Seventh Brain, telepathic discussions with Discordia

Athena's initiative called 'drinks and chat in the garden' was very successful. For a very long time now, the supreme leaders had met in the garden, chiefly for this event. In fact, Athena's gathering was the only approved event while they were still under martial law. Some social drinking was allowed; the drinks were provided by a machine.

As all the leaders were around, Apoll was flaunting his wonderful body as a challenge to all present in the garden to look at him, especially as he was wearing a garment that was absolutely form-fitting.

"So … our discussion was about life. When might we hope to have life on the planet?" He was looked ironically at Herr. "I am quite tired of discussing the organic soup that is so abundant on the planet as long as this organic soup seems to be impotent to produce life, so far."

"Yes, all of us want life on the planet," Prom supported Apoll.

"In that organic soup," Herr shot a condescending look back at Apoll, "the small molecules have started to bond, forming larger and more complex molecules."

"Not good enough to call it life," Athena observed.

"And when will we have life? What does life mean?" Apoll persisted with his skeptical line of questioning.

"When these complex molecules are able to perform assimilation and dissimilation," Prom answered for Herr.

"Yes," Herr said. "Prom is correct. Assimilation and dissimilation means metabolism. Metabolism is the fundamental definition of life."

"I have to admit that it takes an unexpectedly long time," Uran sounded concerned.

"Maybe it isn't possible at all," Gee said, smiling sardonically at Herr.

"Why it should be not possible?" Herr answered back simply. "They've done it in the laboratory countless times."

"Maybe at a planetary scale it just isn't possible," Gee kept his sardonic smile fixed to his face.

"There is absolutely no reason why it's not possible. We diverted meteorites with the right minerals and water to the planet. Now the chemical composition of the planet is perfectly balanced to form and sustain life, " Herr said in a persuasive voice. "It's only a matter of time."

"So much time," Cronn said in a small voice, that only she could hear.

"Time doesn't matter. We are immoral. We have enough time to wait," Afronda stated, in a convinced tone.

For a moment, there was silence in the beautiful garden. The only sound was the water in the cascade.

"Herm, have you picked up any signatures of life on Marr planet or the moons of any nearby planets?" Zeu asked.

Herm had just enough time to shake his head no, before Herr abruptly interrupted them.

"We don't need to pay attention to Marr or any moons. We know even if any elementary life forms developed there, they would not be able to evolve into intelligent life forms."

"Yes," Athena added, "we need to prove that intelligent life forms are able to develop at a planetary scale from inorganics, without any artificial intervention, as if it happened all by itself. Otherwise we'll end up in that stupid, pathetic circle of the chicken and the egg."

"I want huge creatures on this planet," Herr said.

"I want beautiful creatures," Afronda said in low, dreamy voice.

"I want warriors. I want battle. I want war," Arr bellowed. " I am so …" he nearly choked the word out, "… bored."

"Still, I am concerned about this long waiting period. We did not expect this stage to take such a long time," Gee said looking confused. "Herr, are you sure the organic soup has the right composition?"

"Yes …"

But Herr was not able to finish her idea because Hest and Dem entered the garden at that moment. They were accompanied by eight carts floating mid-air on gravitational suspensions. Each cart carried four little children. The children looked around the garden with curious eyes. They were too young to be able to speak fluently, but it was clear to all the leaders from the expressions on their faces that these little children were going to grow into extremely clever adults. They had every opportunity to be highly intelligent, as they were carefully genetically selected and educated by a very special scientific program.

The faces of all the leaders brightened. They began to play with the children, and the children started laughing. Soon, the garden became very noisy. One by one all the children were held by the leaders. It was a wonderful scene to behold. After a long time playing, the children were returned to the floating wagons and they became silent instantly, as if they had received a telepathic command. Four little pairs of eyes were now focused intently on Dem and Hest.

Dem was smiled benignly around the garden to all in attendance.

"Why is there no life yet on the planet?" she asked finally, gazing at Uran.

"We are confident there is going to be life soon," he said. "Only, we incorrectly estimated the amount of time required to form life from inorganics. It is taking much longer than we initially thought."

"There is going to be a little more waiting time," Herr added trying to help Uran.

"How long?" Hest asked in a sharp voice.

"Not very long," Herr answered. "We are going to run new calculations and we will let you know the new estimates soon."

"New estimates ... quite embarrassing! I thought we were able to run the calculations correctly in the first place," Hest smiled to Herr.

"I have to admit, this was unexpected and new calculations need to be run." Zeu said.

"I am more skeptical than that," Dem said. She paused, allowing tension to build all around. "I'm not saying that creating life from inorganics, and then from organics, is impossible. We proved it was possible in our laboratories." She paused and looked around the garden. "There is something wrong."

"Yes," Hest added. "Something is wrong. Poss, are you confident that there are no poisonous chemicals? Some metals that destroy the catalysts of life?"

"Maybe too much arsenic, or mercury or..."

"There are poisons and unwanted metals in the organic soup, but it should still be possible for life to form there," Poss answered in a tiny, shaking voice.

"Then you miscalculated the impact of these poisons on organic molecules!" Dem said, quite upset.

"As we said, we are going to reevaluate the situation and you will have the final report soon," Uran said firmly. "Until then I'll ask all of you to be reasonable." With that he took a step in Dem and Hest's direction, "including you two."

"Very well Uran," Dem answered simply, pivoting. She turned her back on him and at her sign, the floating carts with the children aboard turned and began to glide towards the exit from the garden. Hest remained for a few more seconds, still gazing dispassionately at Uran.

"We trust you. For now," she said in a metallic voice.

Then she turned her back on them all and strode out of the garden.

Discordia stood admiring the huge hologram of the planet, her tall body swaying.

"The planet looks so nice now. Doesn't it?" She addressed the question to her two control room operators.

"Yes, Discordia. Now the planet has sufficient water and the right amount of chemicals. The bombing with ice and mineral asteroids went as scheduled. Also, the planet now has a stable atmosphere."

"And the moon was successfully moved. Now, there is perfect equilibrium. No violent storms, and the day measures 23.7 hours."

"Good. Discordia said in her tiny voice. It was taking such a long time and it was consuming so much energy. Thank you for your hard work."

"The time is not that relevant related to our eternal life, but we definitely needed to recover some energy," John, the dark skinned operator tried to make conversation with Discordia. "We need metals to extend some spatial buildings, uranium for our atomic energy generators and--"

"Stop talking John!" Discordia abruptly interrupted her operator. "I know very well what we need. I sent a detailed report to the supreme leaders. Soon we will know if they will allow us to perform mining operations on this planet. Or, failing that, on the nearby planets or asteroids."

"We had planned to do a great deal with the surrounding asteroids, but since we are a long way from the time of the Big Bang, it might be a challenge if they decide to focus on mining asteroids. Right now this solar system don't see as many asteroids as before. This is good for the planet as the possibility of colliding with a new asteroid is very low right now," added Emm, the fat room operator.

"I expressed this concern in the report already," Discordia said in a grave voice. After a long pause she added, "I won't totally eliminate the possibility of mining asteroids. The leaders might conclude that mining the planet at this scale might leave a footprint and therefore, they might not approve it."

"Yes," John agreed. "The protocol makes it clear that there should be no tracks that might lead the next human beings to discover evidence of our intervention."

"Humans? How do you know human beings will evolve in the end on this planet?" Emm asked

"Intelligent beings, I meant to say," John retorted to Emm.

"The supreme leaders are in a meeting right now. Is it about the mining issue?" Emm asked Discordia.

"Not at all," Discordia answered.

"But we are waiting for an answer regarding the mining ..." John was confused.

Discordia moved her eyes back to the holographic projection, ignoring her operators. John and Emm gazed at each other in puzzlement for a moment.

"Let's watch the meeting then," Emm proposed.

"Video surveillance was forbidden for this meeting," Discordia said, walking around the huge hologram and pretending to study a minor detail on the south pole of the planet.

"It must be something very secret then," Emm concluded.

"Yes indeed," Discordia agreed enigmatically.

"What this meeting about then Discordia?" John asked, walking up to stand close to her.

Discordia's her eyes flitted to John and after a while to Emm. Then she turned back to the hologram. Finally she answered without looking at either one of them, "the meeting is about prokaryotes."

Emm and John stared at each other for a moment.

"Prokaryotes?"

CHAPTER 7

Prokaryotes

You can take power in a blink of the eye. You can lose power in a blink of the eye.

Zeu, Secret Memories

Almost all the leaders were in the meeting room.

"Where is Afronda?" Athena asked.

"Don't worry," Arr said, grinning at Apoll. "She's with Gee. Lesbian stuff," he giggled, looking around at the others.

"Don't be ridiculous!" Athena said in a loud voice.

"We are a free democratic community," Heff observed. "These kinds of things are normal."

"I don't understand their friendship very much," Herr said touching Zeu's leg under the table.

Prom and Poss appeared disturbed by the very subject.

"I guess important things are going to be discussed at this table," Poss said.

"Yes, let's focus on the important issues," Prom agreed.

The door opened and the supreme leaders Uran, Gee

and Cronn stepped in the room, followed at a distance by Afronda.

They took their seats around the table. Afronda took a seat on the right side of the table between Gee and Athena. Also on that side of the table were Apoll, Heff and Arr. Opposite them on the left side of the table, Cronn sat near Herr, Zeu, Poss, Herm and Prom.

Uran smiled politely to the other leaders in the room.

"Nice to see you all again," he said. He took his seat at the head of the table between Gee on his right and Cronn on his left. Beside Gee, Afronda touched her head in a gesture of friendly greeting.

Herr preferred to avoid eye contact with Gee. Her hatred for Gee felt stronger today than all the rest of her days put together, but she wasn't certain why. The depth of emotion was so potent, and yet the cause of it remained elusive.

"It has been some time since we met in this setting in an official meeting, due to the ongoing state of martial law. I have interacted with each of you, individually, regarding the various sub phases of the project, and I would like to congratulate you all on a job well done. Now, however, the time has come for a final evaluation of all we have done for the good on this planet," began Uran. He looked around the room and he smiled benevolently at everyone. "As it seems to have become our custom, I've asked Herm to present a status report. Feel free to address questions or to make statements at any point," he smiled widely at Herm. "The stage is yours, Herm"

"Yes. Thank you Uran," replied Herm, pitching his voice low and sonorously, as though he were about to begin telling a story.

With that, the light in the room dimmed. The atmosphere became almost somber. Dramatically, a hologram of a pale blue ball appeared, hovering just above the center of the table.

"This is the planet as we found it almost two billion years ago. As you can see it is spinning too fast, the moon is too close and ... this ..."

Directly above the planet, a glowing set of graphs, tables and numbers appeared.

"This is the chemical composition of the planet. You can see the chemical elements and their percentage distribution by mass."

"Not enough water," Poss commented.

"Correct," Herm agreed simply and smiled at Poss. "But let's not forget that this projection represents the planet's composition two billion years ago," he paused; looking again at Poss. "Today, however," the hologram of the planet changed to an intense blue, and the moon zipped away to a safer orbit.

"This is the planet and its moon now. Because we reduced the planet's rotation, its day and night cycles total almost 24 hours. The moon is at the correct distance for stabilization of the planet's tides."

"Once intelligent life evolves on the planet, they're going to wonder how the moon ended up over there in precisely the right orbit," Gee observed wryly, smiling around the room.

"All good then," Athena concluded.

"Yes," Gee said, convinced. "With one small exception."

"Which is?" Herr demanded.

"We have lost so much time since our arrival and..."

"We have time," Afronda said jokingly. She smiled to all around the table.

"I don't agree!" Gee said abruptly. She was visibly upset by Afronda's attempt at a joke. All eyes were now fixed on her with grave interest.

"We have lost all contact with our own world. And in all this time they have sent nobody to check on us. Does that not seem strange to you? Maybe we should just leave this planet as it is and go back to our own civilization. Need I remind you, we have spent two billion years here!"

"We have time!" Afronda said, clearly irritated that her close friend Gee had defied her in the front of all the other leaders. "We have to finish the job we were sent here to do, and return with a complete report. We can't return before the mission is completed." Afronda looked imploringly at Gee and continued softly, "I'm sorry Gee, but this is the most important project of my life. I want it to succeed -- as it was designed to do from the very beginning." Afronda surveyed the other leaders seated around the table, looking for support, "I am sure that each of us here is prepared to do whatever it takes to achieve the desired results. Time is just a small piece of the puzzle."

"Afronda..." Gee seemed prepared to argue, but she was interrupted by Uran.

"Okay," Uran said, trying to make peace between the two friends. "Maybe the situation is not as dire as Gee seems to think and Afronda is right."

Afronda directed a smile at Uran.

"However, we must remain vigilant, as the saboteur has still not been found. Perhaps this scenario is exactly what he or she wanted."

"What do you mean?" Herr demanded in a sharp voice.

"I suggested to Uran that this experiment must be accelerated," Cronn said. "We have to finish what we started as soon as possible and to go back to our home planet."

"I disagree!" Zeu retorted sharply.

All eyes in the room turned towards Zeu. He continued in a high voice, "this is a private experiment. This matter is not up for a vote. Our owner may not be here, but his proxies are. Only Dem and Hest can decide if this experiment should be accelerated or not."

"They are the proxies of the owner for administrative matters. For technical issues, I and the other two supreme leaders are in charge," Uran contradicted Zeu.

For a moment, cold silence flooded the room.

"Supposing you are right, how do you propose to... *accelerate* the experiment?" Athena asked after a moment.

"We would have to seed the planet with the correct prokaryotes. Prokaryotes that have been created here, in our lab," Gee said reasonably.

"What?" Prom said, his voice laced with shock. "That would be a terrible breach of protocol!"

"Nobody needs to know," Gee responded calmly.

"Nobody?" Arr said incredulously. "Dem and Hest are watching us right now. They are in charge of this project ..."

"Not exactly." Uran interrupted abruptly.

"What do you mean?" Athena demanded.

"Nobody is able to monitor this meeting right now," Uran assured the others confidently.

"Hest and Dem have the authority to override everything. They most certainly are watching us--" Heff was not able to finish his thought as Gee interrupted him.

"Not anymore. Things change. There cannot be two commanders on this experiment. We have decided that Hest and Dem must be isolated, and we, the supreme the leaders, must take total control." Gee's voice sounded crystal clear and cold.

"Hest and Dem can kill you in an instant. The microchip in your brain is also a little bomb. If they sense something is wrong, they can activate the bomb in your brain by telepathic command." Herr reminded Gee.

"They won't," Uran declared calmly. "We discovered that their plan was to kill every one of us once the experiment was over. Therefore, we have decided to always be one step ahead of them."

He paused to make eye contact with everyone around the table.

"What are you saying?" Herr asked, her voice betraying notes of worry.

"Since they haven't found the saboteur, they are following a protocol called SP, or *the secret protocol*," Cronn said convincingly as he surveyed the room.

"How can you be so sure?" Prom asked, in a hesitant voice.

"We found out about the secret protocol thanks to--" here Uran paused for a moment, "thanks to the one man here in this room who hasn't spoken at all in this meeting, and yet he is here with us in this room."

"Apoll!" Athena demanded, fixing him with a glare. "What do you know about this?" Apoll smiled happily, as though enjoying being the center of attention He was sure everyone in the room was admiring his importance at that moment, as well as his stunning good looks and remarkable physique.

"I am able to infiltrate any software and," he paused here for effect, "… any *secret protocol*.

"And has already done astonishing things for us in this meeting," Uran smiled knowingly at Apoll.

"Hest and Dem are now watching a record of this meeting that I prepared in advance," he announced proudly to the room, searching their faces for approval. "Right about now they are watching us checking the planet's chemical composition and estimating when the first prokaryotes will begin to form." Uran was absolutely sure about everything.

"And that is exactly what we *should* be doing!" Afronda said firmly.

"Afronda, dear …" Gee said in a voice dripping with compassion. "You seem not to understand the full significance of our situation." Gee looked pityingly at Afronda. "There is a saboteur on this ship. He is very diabolical, and so far nobody has been able to catch him. The possibility that he will never be found is very high. Therefore, it would be foolish not to assume that Dem and Hest will resort to the SP sooner or later." Gee seemed concerned at Afronda's lack of understanding, "in other words, they are going to kill everyone here in this room, along with the saboteur." Gee paused to survey the table.

"If there really is a secret protocol, then why haven't Dem and Hest already used it?" Afronda was grasping at straws.

"They haven't used it *yet*," Gee pointed out, trying to convince Afronda and the other leaders in the room.

"And they won't use it," Afronda continued calmly. "If they kill us, how will they finish the experiment?"

"Don't be naive!" Cronn bellowed. "They don't need us! They have an abundance of DNA in their bank. They can create as many life forms as they need, and exactly the kind they need. And don't forget about the young students."

"Ah. It turns out that even on the matter of creating new life forms, they have a secret," Gee said looking intently around the room. "Their true mission is to create a super being; an individual that will be superior even to us. What they fail to grasp is that once created, such super intelligent being cannot be controlled," she cried. "They are fools!"

The room was plunged into cold silence.

"So the real question is, How can we eliminate Hest and Dem without losing our own lives?" Prom asked.

Uran reassured the leaders, "as Apoll explained, they're seeing a decoy meeting of us right now. We can use this strategy in the future when we meet. The most important part is that once we leave this meeting, we act normally. If we do that, Dem and Hest will know nothing."

"In the meantime," continued Gee, "we have to do everything we can to accelerate this experiment, including seeding the planet with synthesized prokaryotes. But we must be careful not to make any mistakes! If they catch us in a mistake they will kill us at all, and even Apoll won't be able to save us. This plan will succeed if there are no further mistakes, and once the experiment is all done, we can go back home alive, and return as people who conducted a successful experiment."

"I still don't agree with the plan to seed the planet with prokaryotes," Afronda protested.

"Why not?" Gee asked incredulously. "It will accelerate this experiment dramatically, and nudge it in the direction we want, I might add."

"Because I want to see life forming from inorganic molecules on this planet for myself," Afronda said simply, imploring the other leaders for support.

"But it's been accomplished so many times in the lab," Gee argued.

"Exactly. And for that reason alone, this experiment is unique. It is supposed to take the laboratory results of creating life from inorganic molecules and apply it on a planetary scale." Afronda was trying to convince the other leaders. "And, most importantly, it must do so without any intervention from us."

Uran shook his head, "but we have already intervened. We stabilized the planet. We bombarded it with asteroids specially selected for their chemical composition. We moved the orbit of the planet's moon. And so on. I would call that a massive intervention in the planet's evolution."

"But that was all as per the experiment's description. That was allowed as per the initial protocol," Afronda shot back. "It was accepted because it was intervention only at the *inorganic* level. The formation of life is a very delicate matter. Once the planet is in its organic phase, it must be in total quarantine." She looked around the room, "all of you must understand this."

"No matter," Gee concluded, overriding Afronda. "We will put it to a vote. All those in favor of seeding the planet with prokaryotes?"

And, smiling smugly at the others, confident of the result, Gee raised her hand. She darted her eyes toward

Cronn who raised his hand as well. But as she surveyed the others, her confident smile froze on her face. In the room only three hands were up: hers, Cronn's and Uran's.

"What's the matter with you people?" Gee shouted. "Your life is threatened and instead of rushing to save yourselves, you ..." she floundered, unable to finish.

"We volunteered for this experiment," Afronda said calmly. "We have the time to follow it through each stage, and--"

But she had no time to continue as Gee had immobilized her in an expert fighting hold. With unmatched speed, Gee held her fingers skillfully against Afronda's throat. One tiny movement and Afronda would be dead. "The rest of you had better agree to the prokaryote plan," Gee was shrieking now, "otherwise I will not hesitate to kill her!"

Everyone in the room stood up. For an instant that seemed longer than an eternity, they tried to decide what to do.

Afronda took advantage of Gee's moment of inattention and, with an extremely quick motion, lashed out with her fingers at Gee's hand. The hit was strong and sure and hit its mark, taking Gee by surprise, and creating a momentary paralysis in Gee's hand. In that fraction of a second, Afronda jumped out of Gee's immobilizing grasp.

"I have new fighting skills now Gee. Skills you are not aware of," Afronda crouched low and ready in a combat position, prepared for next Gee's attack. Fear coursed through her veins as she thought about Gee's reputation as a terrifying fighter.

With a lightning-quick move, Herr leaped over the table

and thrust herself between Gee and Afronda. The next instant, she attacked Gee, screaming, "I'll kill you, bitch!"

"Stand back!" Zeu roared.

Herr moved back a few steps. Gee did the same.

"Just a few words," Zeu commanded. "After this display, you three cannot continue to be our supreme leaders. You must agree to the new reality: you are no longer our supreme leaders. If you agree, we will consider sparing your lives."

"And if we do not agree?" Uran asked, taking up a threatening combat position.

Gee and Cronn also shifted to offensive combat positions.

"We know you three are ferocious fighters," Zeu looked back at the others. Herr, Athena and Afronda were already in combat formation against Gee. The rest of the leaders were preparing for the fight too. Finally Zeu moved his eyes back to Uran.

"If you don't agree, we cannot let you leave this room alive."

———————⬦———————

"I can't believe you did it without telling me."

Afronda was angry. Her face was red. She, the master of dissimulation, was for once paying no attention to people around her. There in the beautiful garden, all the leaders had gathered in loose white robes. Just a few hours ago they had all been covered in blood after their fight with the three supreme leaders. They had barely had enough time to bathe and have the medical robots attend to their wounds. Still, a few of them bore signs from the battle on their bodies.

Afronda was very sure by now that her elusive

premonition that her life was in grave danger had been about this fight. If she hadn't studied the fighting arts with Athena and Arr, she would have been dead by now. And she still couldn't believe Apoll had played such a double-crossing role in the conflict.

"I warned you to do nothing without informing me. Why you didn't listen to me?" Afronda raised her voice at Apoll.

"Can't we discuss this later?" Apoll shot back in a bored voice.

"Later? Dem and Hest are on their way here. I'm not sure there will even be a later for you."

"We'll see," Apoll answered calmly.

"I would defend you, if you told me why you did it," Afronda tried to be very convincing.

"He seduced me."

"Wh-- … what?" Afronda's face turned a darker shade of red.

"You have to face the fact that I have sex with other people too. Not just with you or your replica."

Afronda threw a loaded look at Arr as if to say, *this guy is so naive, who the hell does he think in this universe only has sex with one person over all this time?*

But Afronda never managed to articulate that thought. Instead she asked, "still, how do you go from being seduced to committing criminal acts?"

"I appreciate that you want to defend me, Afronda, but I assure you I can defend myself."

Athena come close to him and said in a low voice, "I don't think you fully understand your situation, Apoll."

"I don't think you are aware of the whole picture,

Athena," Apoll shot back. Athena gazed at him intently. Suddenly she started to make other mental projections and interpretations.

He might be right. I don't think he would ever dare go against Dem and Hest. Which means Dem and Hest have been manipulating this whole bloody situation…

She was not able to finish her toughs, as Dem and Hest stepped into the garden.

"I can't believe this is happening," Discordia said in her tiny voice. It was easy to distinguish the anger in her voice.

"Yes," John said. He was quite terrified, which made his skin appear to be much darker.

"It has been almost seven hours since we lost control of the ship," noted Emm, the fat control room operator.

"At least all life support systems are functioning normally," John added.

"It's the emergency protocol," Discordia advised. "Dem and Hest must have initiated the emergency protocol. I don't understand why they didn't inform me, though … this is killing me," she sighed.

Dem and Hest stepped into the garden. They gazed at the people gathered there with cold eyes. They settled themselves on the two massive seats made of white rock with all the leaders standing in front of them. For a moment, it was silent in the beautiful garden. Only the trickle of the water in the cascade broke the silence.

"The emergency protocol has been initiated," Hest said in a metallic voice.

"Only the life support systems will function normally. The other systems will remain under our control," Dem said in dominating tone. She looked at all the leaders one by one. Finally her gaze settled and she graced Apoll with a smile.

"Thanks for your cooperation, Apoll."

Apoll bent his head in a gesture of submission.

The rest of the leaders looked around at each other perplexed. Afronda was particularly shaken and decided never to underestimate Apoll or his cunning again.

"What exactly … happened?" asked Herr.

"We were manipulated, if I understand correctly," Athena interjected.

"We found ourselves faced with a dangerous situation," Dem said. "You see, we discovered that Uran, Gee and Cronn were the ones who sabotaged the star gate devices, but we didn't have enough evidence to prove their guilt, so we had to act."

Dem surveyed the leaders and addressed a small, reassuring smile at them, "but that was only temporary."

"How can that even be possible?" Afronda asked. "I thought you were able to monitor everything that happens on this ship."

"We are." Hest said, "which is why they sabotaged the star gates before the ship was even launched. With our currently available tools it was quite impossible to detect the malfunction they implanted in the SGs." Dem said.

"Their plan was quite diabolical," Hest continued, "the star devices were in position and able to function within normal limits, until we came very close to the threshold destination."

"Then, when we approached the destination, they activated the critical bug, causing the SG elements to malfunction and send out out an auto-destroy signal to all previously launched SGs."

"And how did you determine that the supreme leaders did it?" Heff asked. He was clearly making an effort to stand up, but his deformed body didn't help him.

Dem and Hest were looking for a moment to each other largely smiling.

"Think about it. Everyone in this crew volunteered for this mission. Every last one of you, that is, but the supreme leaders," Hest smiled knowingly to the remaining leaders.

"We suspect they arranged the original sabotage in a way that was undetectable to us. To prove their guilt, we decided to give them a chance to do it again in order to clearly prove their guilt."

"To … to do it again?" Prom asked, quite confused.

"Yes. Compared to those of you who volunteered for this mission regardless of the long duration, for the supreme leaders this was just a job. They were motivated to make the mission as short as possible," Dem said.

"Seeding the planet with manufactured prokaryotes would shorted the mission considerably," Hest continued convincingly, "and would guarantee the results expected by the owner. Therefore, the supreme leaders would earn their contractual benefit plus a considerable bonus."

"But weren't they the littlest bit curious about how this experiment would proceed at a planetary scale?" Herm wondered.

"Who, Gee? That calculating bitch?" Herr's voice rose. "I used to be friends with her at one time. Except for her own income, nothing was interesting to her. Nothing! It is a shame that creatures like her still exist in the universe." Herr was very angry now.

For a few seconds there was silence in the garden, except for the trickle of the water falling in the cascade. It was a good time for the leaders to make up their minds.

"What's next then?" Zeu asked.

"You will be the new supreme leader." Dem said.

"And Herr will be your deputy. There will be only one deputy and not two as before." Hest continued.

The air in the beautiful garden seemed to shimmer with uncertaintly.

"I should ... think about this ..." Zeu said in a voice that betrayed his confusion.

"Don't tell me you are not interested having such great power for yourself," Hest said mockingly.

"Aren't we supposed to vote? I mean, democracy, and all that stuff," Herr added. "We need to know if the leaders want us to be their supreme leaders."

"Need we remind you that this ship doesn't belong to you! It is our owner's property. Choosing the supreme leaders is the exclusive responsibility of the owner's proxies. That means the decision rests solely with Dem and me. This is more a technocracy than a democracy. In other matters you may use the voting democracy standard to arrive at a decision."

Dem took over for Hest, "therefore, do not confound democracy with technocracy. Our first priority is to make sure the ship is in good hands and to ensure its return to our owner in good working order. We need to preserve the capital enclosed in this ship. This is primarily a matter of protecting capital. One last time, if there is a gross misunderstanding, a major internal conflict, or similar, not only the ship, but all our lives could be in peril. Therefore, we need to make sure the supreme leaders are aligned with us -- on the owner's side. We are the only ones empowered to appoint them. You know this very well."

Dem and Hest looked around the garden.

"We were all prepared to conduct this mission without external help from the very beginning. The experiment began some time ago when we first stabilized the planet, and we are going to continue it until it is concluded. We will finish the experiment and we will keep detailed records of all data for our owner as initially intended.

"In conclusion, there will be no lab-manufactured prokaryotes! One of the most important steps in this experiment is to see if intelligent life can indeed be created from inorganic molecules on a planetary scale," Dem's voice rang out crystal clear in the garden.

"Athena, you are going to make sure no prokaryotes, DNA or other organics are sent to the planet, even in error," Hest gazed at Athena, who bent her head in acknowledgement of the order.

"Herm, make sure no asteroid with some potential organics comes near planet," Dem added.

"We have before us a beautiful blue planet," Hest said pausing between each word for emphasis.

Dem looked around at all the leaders again. Suddenly a holographic projection of the blue planet materialized between Dem, Hest and the leaders. All of them observed the hologram with enormous interest.

Taking a deep breath Dem said, "this planet will give us the answers to questions that our very advanced civilization has not been able to ascertain until now. Our civilization needs these answers. And this planet is going to give them to us."

CHAPTER 8

Elementary life

*Sometimes we naturally make
embarrassing mistakes.*

Afronda, Team discussions

Discordia was so very pleased with Zeu because he gave her authority as a full leader. *Uran and his helpers deserve what they have accomplished*, Discordia was thinking. *They were unable to understand my valuable role on this mission.* Also she was furious with herself for not being able to find the saboteurs despite running scenario after scenario through her powerful mind. She smiled to her room operators. *In fact, what I should expect from a saboteur?* Discordia was not able to stop her negative thoughts about Uran, Gee and Cronn. She was embarrassed to admit that she regretted that their lives had been spared. *That stupid protocol,* she thought. The protocol required mercy: transgressors were not to be killed, only stripped of all rank and to have their minds reprogrammed to a very basic, domestic level. *Animal level*, she said to herself.

"We can manage things here ma'am," Emm said.

"You should go attend the leaders meeting," John suggested admiringly.

"I won't attend this meeting," Discordia answered in a tiny voice.

"But … all the leaders are invited," Emm insisted.

"Zeu knows I have a primary role in the success of this mission. That's why he acknowledged me as a full leader," Discordia responded with great pride.

"That's precisely why you should attend this scheduled meeting. It starts in ten minutes."

"I will attend the next meeting. Right now, I have other priorities; things that I would rather manage personally," Discordia was enigmatic.

"We are more than happy to help you Ma'am."

"What can we do to help?" John and Emm prodded.

Discordia sent a telepathic command and the huge wall in front of them became totally transparent. Now they had visual contact with the planet. It looked like an immense blue ball.

"Why we don't have organic life there yet?" Discordia lamented.

"I think it's simply a matter of philosophy, ma'am."

"How is that?" She turned to John, ready to argue.

"There," John gestured at the planet with his head, "are very big organic molecular associations ma'am."

"They almost can mimic the assimilation and de-assimilation processes ma'am. And that means metabolism," Emm added, convinced.

"And metabolism means life," John finished, but his

voice became rather interrogative as he saw by the look on Discordia's face that she didn't agree.

"That's Herr's theory," Discordia said, with a dismissive wave of her hand.

John and Emm watched her, perplexed. Discordia stalked alongside the huge transparent wall.

"Then please, teach us Discordia. What should life mean?"

"Or look like?"

Discordia turned her back to the transparent wall and faced the operators. She was not pleased with their line of questioning.

"What a question!" she said with a reproachful look.

"When we were on our home planets, or near them, how did we know if there was life in other solar systems or galaxies? And by life, I mean at least prokaryotes?"

"We scan them with our telescopes to determine if the planet is within the optimal orbital range around its star; what we call the 'life ring'," John tried to guess.

"You started well," Discordia was still disappointed.

"We scan the planet for life?" John tried again.

"Correct! This is our current case. We know this planet, and Marr's planet as well, are in the life ring. But we still need a confirmed life signal from the planet on the ship's scanners. Only when that signal goes ON, can we officially declare that the planet has life."

"Yes, you are right Discordia! That is the definition of a planet with life. A living planet," Emm marveled.

Discordia looked around the room, "and I am going to check the ship's life scanners myself."

Now that martial law was over, the ship's residents could enjoy many freedoms. All the leaders and the members of their teams were free to walk whenever they wanted on the huge special ship without restrictions. They were able to meet in groups as large as they wanted. This was a release even for Arr and his team as they didn't have to focus so much of their attention on monitoring other people, the ship, and its activities.

They were also allowed to travel to the planet on small ships. However, they needed the approval of Athena and her team prior to any trip. Under their expert supervision each ship was carefully checked to make sure it was well sealed and there would be no possibility of inadvertently contaminating the planet with DNA.

Zeu and Herr sat at the head of the table to steer the meeting of the supreme leaders. They had steered several meetings by now, and had proved that they have exceptional leadership skills. However, they still faced a terrible dilemma: there had been no confirmation of life on the planet yet, and they worried that their time was running out before Dem and Hest would lose patience and issue a new replacement order. This stage was taking such an unexpectedly long time!

Zeu and Herr looked around the table for the other leaders' input.

"Discordia said she cannot attend this meeting. She sent her apologies to all," Zeu mentioned.

"We haven't received a clear life signal from the planet, and she is so very frustrated," Herr added.

"Yes! Why are there no prokaryotes? Why is there no life yet on the planet?" Zeu asked accusingly.

"We will get the life signal soon," Herr added calmly.

"Soon? How soon?" Zeu's volume increased.

The leaders around the table were a little bit intimidated by his anger.

"Very soon," Herr answered keeping her voice calm. "Sonner than you expect," She added, gazing at Poss.

"Yes," Poss added, unsure if she was asking him to step in the discussion. "As I mentioned initially," Poss tried to adjust his voice to a normal level so as not to disturb Zeu, "I am concerned about the high levels of arsenic compounds and the chemical reactions induced by them. The computers are running many possible arsenic scenarios, unfortunately, they have not yet been able to determine if arsenic levels have inhibited the formation of life."

"How can life evolve in a poison soup?" Prom wondered.

Herr shot a very critical look at Prom.

"Complex organic molecular reactions are already metabolizing the arsenic compounds. Very soon the metabolized arsenic compounds will not be harmful for life," Herr somewhat contradicted Poss and Prom's theory.

"Metabolism…" Zeu wondered. "If there is metabolism, that should mean life! So why haven't we received the life signal from the planet?" His voice became even louder, and the leaders began to sense some anger creeping into it.

"As I said," Herr was immensely calm, "in my opinion, life does exist on the planet already." She paused, looking around the room. "It is simply a matter of concentration. There just isn't a high enough concentration of prokaryotes able to generate the positive life signal on our ship's life detection sensors."

"That's a reasonable explanation," Prom tried to help Herr.

"I can present you some time estimates based on the current prokaryote concentration--" Poss tried, before being abruptly interrupted by Zeu.

"You've already done so several times and you were wrong! According to your projections we were supposed to have seen life several hundred years ago! Why should we believe your new estimates?"

"Maybe we should set the life scanners to ultrasensitive search," Athena suggested.

Afronda appeared to be on Zeu's side, "maybe it's something else? I don't know … mercury … selenium? They both act as poisons to life…" She trailed off and looked at Poss. "Did you run sufficient tests to confirm that all possible poison compounds are under the threshold level?"

After a sharp intake of breath, Prom hissed, "yes, of course I did--" but he was not able to finish his sentence.

"Priority zero!" Discordia's tinny voice echoed around the room.

Now that he was a supreme leader, Uran seemed to react badly to this interruption. On the contrary, Zeu always acknowledged Discordia as a very important leader. He appreciated her suggestions and took them into consideration. He answered her in a normal voice, "we are listening, Discordia."

"Thank you sir." Discordia said. She seemed to struggle to catch her breath before quickly blurting, "we have received the life signal from the planet on our scanners sir!"

Elementary life on the planet! This was a reason to celebrate. The large ball room on the ship was rarely used. It was massively large by its own rights, but the wall-less technology made it seem quite infinite. Dotted around the room were little tables with splendid floral arrangements. The protocol robots served drinks in glasses with complex and beautiful shapes that changed according to the kind of drink requested.

The leaders were each permitted to bring several members from their crew to the first hour of the party, with the rest of the crew being allowed to join after that. Each leader brought three or four team members. As each of them had 32 team members, there were long discussions regarding who should be the primary representative at the party. Afronda was the only leader to overstep the guidelines. She brought seven members of her team; all of them male. She was dressed in a very sheer white dress that was fitted tightly on her upper body with a very loose skirt. Her seven male guests wore identical fitted suits with tight black pants. The suit jackets were worn open with no shirts underneath, allowing all to see their wonderfully muscled chests. The seven men stayed close to Afronda, creating a stark contrast that showed off her beauty to even greater effect. There was a general ohh… when she stepped in the ballroom. Everyone admired her and her attendants.

The leaders hardly knew the members from the other teams as they didn't come in touch with each other very often. Each team always pretended that they were busy with their dedicated team research.

Athena was dressed a loose white gown that showed off her muscular arms. She brought with her a man and a woman, each dressed in white robes that coordinated perfectly with Athena's. The woman who accompanied Athena came very close to her and covered her mouth with her hand to keep the computers from reading her lips. In a soft voice she said to Athena, "everyone one on Afronda's team is handsome. Maybe even Apoll."

Athena turned her face to her and she said, "true. Afronda is our mistress of beauty. I am so proud of her."

Apoll was dressed in a white suit and white pants, his curly blond hair flowing down to his shoulders. Four very beautiful young ladies accompanied him; each wearing identical pink dresses, long and sheer enough to show off their beautiful bodies. Despite his attractive entourage, however, Apoll couldn't stop himself from admiring Afronda's all-male retinue.

Herr stood with her guests, a man and a woman. She couldn't suppress a smile at Apoll's admiration of Afronda's guests. *Apoll boy,* she thought, *you're not doing a very good job of hiding your interest in those boys.*

Arr had invited three men and one woman from his team. Each of them had over-developed muscles, and two of the men looked like identical twins. The twins' heads were shaved, and the other man's long blond hair was held back in a ponytail. The muscular woman had long black hair that she wore down, flowing to her elbows. All three were dressed in tight black outfits made of a leather-like material. They almost looked like fighting costumes.

"I didn't expect Prom to attend the party," Arr confessed to his guests. "He said he doesn't like parties".

Poss was fashionably dressed in a light aqua costume.

Like water, thought Athena. She couldn't explain why

she always felt like had to compete with Poss. Near him two beautiful ladies in fashionable light green clothes looked around the ball room, smiling in a friendly manner at everyone.

As usual, Heff stood out due to his deformed body. He wore a very nice black costume that was a little bit large to camouflage his deformed body. The overall effect was that he looked quite decently dressed. He was with two ladies dressed in long black robes and two gentlemen dressed in similar black costumes to his. They were beautiful people, but they didn't appear too friendly.

Discordia also stood out with her two operators compared to the beautiful people in the room. She was too tall and too slim. As usual, she wore a very tight long dress that fitted her body too closely. Her operators John and Emm were dressed in very fashionable black costumes. Despite the fact that their bodies were not very beautiful, the clothing made them look handsome enough.

Prom was also at the party. He was dressed in a black and white costume and he was accompanied by two ladies who were arrayed all in white. His muscled body contrasted somewhat with his two guests, who were quite skinny.

"All right." Zeu began in a strong voice. "Thank you everyone for coming," his muscular body was covered by a dark robe. Near him were four extremely beautiful women dressed in fashionable dark gowns.

Zeu paused as Herm stepped into the ballroom, dressed in very tight white clothes. He was accompanied by four attractive men. As they were a little bit late they walked quickly in Zeu's direction.

Everyone in the ballroom now moved closer to hear

Zeu, "As you know, we have received a signal on the ship's scanners confirming elementary life on the planet. That means life has reached the threshold level where we can now designate the planet as a life planet." He looked proudly around the room. "Herr and I decided this was good reason to celebrate. We have good food: not the kind of jellied food we eat daily I mean--"

The people in the room started laughing as it was a good, entertaining joke. Zeu paused to enjoy this happy moment and continued. "We also have very good wine and alcohol tonight. We have decided to waive restrictions tonight regarding alcohol consumption."

Again people laughed. "Now I'll have Poss, our main chemical mind, explain how organics can form life on a planet that was totally barren of life before," he turned his eyes to Poss. "Poss: you have the floor."

"Thank you Zeu," Poss said.

All eyes turned to Poss and it became obvious that his long aqua robe was actually a combination of green and blue. In the bright light, the blue reflections were dazzling. His four female attendants were dressed in the same material. Afronda couldn't stop admiring their beauty and their stunningly fashionable dresses.

"In the beginning," Poss began, "we had nothing but inorganics."

In the middle of the large ballroom a hologram appeared, showing molecular chemical models, percentages, and also the time line.

"As there was abundant inorganic carbon, it began to combine mainly with hydrogen, creating organic molecules. Do not forget that this is how we got oxygen and nitrogen.

With the help of electricity from lightning and high heat from volcanic activity, it was only a matter of time until we got amino acids." He paused to give time to people to check the chemistry and the timeline in the hologram.

"Finally complex proteins developed on the planet, and protein associations enabled by elementary assimilation and dissimilation. At this stage, we refer to it as metabolism. Herr?"

Herr smiled around, delicately adjusting her extravagant gown, and picked up the story where Poss left off.

"Once we have metabolism, we have life. Our high-resolution cameras proved there are now microscopic life forms on the planet. They are unicellular life forms. A few samples were submitted to my lab. There is no doubt they are prokaryotes. And they are present at high enough concentrations on the planet for the life signal to be received by our scanners."

She smiled and directed her eyes to Zeu expectantly, "so let's have a nice party for these sexy prokaryotes!" he cheered.

All the people in the room screamed in unison, "hurrah!"

Glasses with sparkling champagne were passed out to the guests quickly by hovering robotic devices. There was a general happiness in the room.

Near Athena, her male companion leaned close to her and said, "I can't see Dem and Hest. That must mean--"

"My dear friend," Athena interrupted him, "let's forget our classical analysis for tonight and get drunk."

Dem and Hest ate a light dinner composed mainly by vegetables and some fish. They decided to have only water during and after dinner. Comfortably seated in their massage chairs, they carefully watched the holographic projection. It showed a great deal of chemical data. There were very complex molecules, lots of numbers and descriptive terminology. On the dynamic hologram, many molecules were combined resulting in amino acids, and finally complex proteins. The holographic projection also showed the proteins combining in the first single-celled life forms.

"This is not a theory, anymore, Hest. This is already history," Dem smiled to Hest.

"Yes dearest Dem. Today is a great day. We have the proof that there is life on the planet. Our owner should be very pleased with us." Hest smiled back to Dem. "In summary, from the basic inorganic elements of carbon, hydrogen, oxygen and nitrogen, we have proved that in time, we can create life. It has now been proven on a planetary scale."

"True," Hest acknowledged.

"So … they are on the right track. We can also admit that Zeu has turned out to be a good leader."

"Yes, he has proved he can handle the program … until …" Hest paused deliberately. "Until a certain point."

"I hope for him that point is far in the future," Den sipped water from her glass. "And now, since their experiment is going in the right direction, we should pay close attention to ours."

Without needing to answer, Hest sent a telepathic command to the main computer. From the room's floor a container cylinder containing a naked brain appeared.

The brain was floating in a semitransparent liquid.

From the bottom of the brain delicate wire connections were going down to the container's base. Around the brain few bubbles were flouting it the top of the container.

"We are listening you, brain number seven." Hest said.

"I'm afraid I don't have too much to tell you." The brain's voice sounded calm coming from the room's concealed speakers.

"Why is that?" Dem demanded in a hard voice.

"They are very little children. The telepathic interpretation of their thoughts is difficult. The process to extend their lives eternally has resulted in an advanced period of childhood. They can't even speak yet!" The voice in the speakers sounded like it was crying.

"But they can certainly think," Hest interrupted him abruptly.

"Yes, but their thoughts are inconsistent. Sometimes they take the form of words, other times they are mere perceptions, impressions without connection, or … something in between."

"We don't care. We asked you to use your telepathic abilities together with our computer's electronic abilities to read their minds. We want the final report."

"I have it," The voice in the speakers seemed to be making an effort to appear calm. "It was difficult to determine how to present the final data to you," the brain continued in the same calm voice, but the number of the bubbles increasing around it betrayed its anxiety. Hest had to suppress the smile on her face, *he is certainly thinking intensely*.

"What did you chose then?" Dem shot back.

"I prepared a record in a holographic projection. There is the room with all the children and the babysitter robots.

When you look at a child, words will appear above its head. These words represent the thoughts, impressions, and perceptions that I was able to detect and the computers were able to interpret."

"Perfect!" Dem said. "You are free to go now."

"One more thing," Hest said. "This is highly confidential. Don't share this with your closest friend, Discordia."

"Yes ma'am. I fully understand this and I will conform. Regarding the thoughts, please understand the limitations, and do not expect to see complex sentences there. This will come as the children mature."

"The rest is not your problem. We have our own ways of handling this."

Dem smiled broadly in the direction of the brain direction and said, "thanks again. You can go now." The container with the brain disappeared back into the floor.

Once alone, Dem and Hest gazed at each other momentarily, as if to say, "are you ready?" And then they started to mentally connect and work with their computers.

"I can't believe that brain number seven didn't taking into consideration that once the kids are mature enough, some of them might be able to hide their deeper thoughts. That's why we have to do this now."

"Absolutely! That's why now is the time for the good and right interpretation of their thoughts. It is of paramount importance for us."

"Let's see…"

In the middle of the room the hologram showed the 32 children in their little beds ready to sleep.

The perfect moment to read their minds, Dem thought.

Randomly, they fixed their eyes on different children.

Instantly words appeared on the hologram. As Dem and Hest moved their eyes from one child to another they saw little sentences like:

"Maybe I should have more milk."

"Zeu … what a big man."

"Apoll is so nice."

"Too tired. I need sleep."

At the same moment, Dem and Hest both pointed their eyes to the little bed with a number 13 above it. Instantly the words appeared above the bed.

"I want to change the world."

Dem's water glass smashed on the floor as it slipped from her hand in shock

"It is not too late! Let's kill him!" Hest said. Her voice was trembling.

CHAPTER 9

The mega continent

Great things request great effort.

Athena

Discordia bent her tall body to address Zeu. "Please say yes!" she said in a tiny imploring voice.

She spent twenty minutes standing up and walking around the holographic presentation. She did her best and her control room operators John and Mann helped her from time to time. She had presented him with ample data, but still Zeu appeared unconvinced.

Now, once the hologram disappeared, the room appeared quite empty. As tall she was, Discordia towered over Zeu. Behind her, Discordia's operators stood. John was not able to control the sweat glistening on his dark skin. He was quite terrified to stand directly in front of Zeu for so long. Emm was also quite strained. It appeared to take a great effort to sustain his fat body. Zeu was the only one seated. He reclined in a large chair, or throne as he preferred to call it.

"Sometimes I regret being such a brutal person," He said in a very loud and terrifying voice. "I would like to offer you platitudes about the quality of your presentation, which was incidentally quite a good one and so on, but the final answer is still no. Imagine that I turned you down kindly and without humiliating you."

For a moment there was a terrible silence in the room. Emm felt like his heart was beating too loud and Zeu must be able to hear it.

"But everything makes sense," Discordia tried to protest.

"Silence!" Zeu shouted. He took a deep breath and then barked out an order, "Jon, Emm: out." The two were happy to leave the room.

"Do you understand—woman—what you are asking?"

"My presentation was very logical. I fully understand the consequences. I am asking permission to create a mega continent colliding all the volcanic islands."

"It will waste so much energy."

"We can mine the planet afterwards, and rebuild all that we wasted. We can also--" Discordia's tiny voice continued without hesitation.

"Silence!" Zeu bellowed again. "Now I understand why Uran never allowed you to attend his meetings! This had better be the first and last time you dare to defy me. If you do it again, there will be seriously bad consequences for you. Now go away."

For a moment, Discordia stood before Zeu, stretching to her full height. Finally, she bent her body in acquiescence.

"Sir," she turned and left the room.

Outside, John and Emm tried to console her.

"You did everything possible, ma'am."

"Don't let this upset you." They walked along the huge corridor. "There will be other big projects--"John started to say but suddenly Discordia stopped in her tracks. She turned to face him.

"Who told you this project is canceled?"

⸺◆⸺

The four ladies were looking at the planet through the glass wall. All of them were dressed in very fashionable gowns.

"Look at this beauty," Afronda said. She was discreetly analyzing the other ladies. "It is a gigantic lovely blue ball."

"We are lucky because there are no clouds right now and we have a wonderful view of the planet." Discordia completed Afronda's thought. She was wearing a very tight black dress in the latest fashion, which made her look even taller and skinnier than usual.

"Now that there's some oxygen on the planet," Athena observed, "the atmosphere might be breathable soon."

"Yes," Herr concurred. "Don't forget, it's been almost two thousand billion years since life first formed. Now the planet has mega colonies of lifeforms able to perform photosynthesis. They are combining carbon from carbon dioxide and hydrogen from water into hydrocarbons. The energy they use is solar radiation, or sunlight. They use carbon dioxide and release molecular oxygen."

"Yes," Athena said, "some of the oxygen already reacted with iron and other metals. This was important to purify the atmosphere."

"In fact the year zero should be the year when we first detected life on this planet," Herr said in a convinced voice.

"I am sure Herm would disagree with you," Discordia said in an apologetic tone.

Still, Herr turned to her quite angry. As though she hadn't noticed Herr's reaction, Discordia approached the glass wall and stood close to it. "For Herm, year zero is the year the planet is born."

"Actually, year zero is the moment of the Bing Bang." Athena said.

"We're referring to a planetary timeline Athena. For Herm year zero begins at the time of the formation of the planet. For Herr, year zero begins with the appearance of life. What about you, Afronda?" Discordia questioned in her tiny voice.

"For me, year zero is the year when we finally have beautiful creatures on this planet," Afronda said. She was very certain of her definition. "I refer, of course, to humanoid creatures. We haven't reached my year one yet. " She smiled at the three ladies.

"And for you Discordia?"

As though disturbed from her careful examination of the blue ball Discordia turned her back to the glass wall. Now she was standing up and as tall as she was she was looking down to the three ladies.

"I am sure you don't want to know my answer."

"What do you mean?" Herr said in an angry voice.

"Well ... however," Discordia appeared unsettled. She paused deliberately, "... if you insist ..." she paused again gazing at each of them one by one.

For me, year zero will be the year when a mega-continent is formed."

Afronda started laughing. Discordia turned to Afronda, surprised.

"Dearest Afronda, I'm surprised that you fail to realize the importance of a mega-continent on this planet."

"I utterly disagree, in fact," Afronda said. "When beautiful humans appear on this planet, I am going to be their God of beauty."

"No doubt," Discordia said.

"What could be more beautiful human creatures living on an isolated island and seeing me rising naked from the sea foam?"

"If there is a mega-continent, there will be large coastlines. The people will be well connected and the news of your beauty will spread easily far and wide across the continent. If there are only volcanic islands however, do you imagine yourself jumping from one island to another to share your story?"

"She is quite correct," Athena admitted. "Without a mega-continent, the people will be very isolated as the distance between islands will be too great for their rudimentary ships."

"And even before that," Discordia addressed Herr now, "it will be easy for you to extend or exterminate unwanted mammal populations as you wish. Otherwise it might be difficult to make these changes one by one across many isolated islands." Discordia looked with sympathy at Herr.

"True," Herr admitted simply.

"However, for me, this planet will never have a time of origin because there will never be a mega-continent,"

Discordia said with immense sadness in her voice as she turned to gaze out the window at the immense blue ball of the planet.

Afronda come close to Discordia.

"Why has Zeu refused you so totally?"

Discordia turned her sad face Afronda and made a helpless gesture.

Sadly, Afronda smiled toward Discordia.

"What do you think Athena?"

Athena walked graciously in front of the four men.

Poss always hated this corner of the garden. There were no plants, no water; he felt that there was no humidity at all. There was just sand, rocks and a few tall white columns. He couldn't understand why Athena chose to invite them to this corner of the garden. Being far from water was so hard for him. He felt like he hated Athena for this.

Heff decided to sit on a big rock. All the others were dressed in white robes with an ample low-cut neck allowing their muscular bodies to be seen. Athena herself had a well-muscled body. Heff was dressed in a large black robe without the low-cut neck the others wore.

Arr and Prom were watching Athena's careful steps.

"With all due respect, I don't think you stand a chance of convincing me, Athena. I like the planet as it is now: a blue ball," Poss said firmly.

"With a mega-continent, the planet will still be a blue ball," Athena smiled broadly at Poss and the others. " It's easy to run some elementary calculations and understand that the mega continent will cover only just a little bit more than a quarter of the planet's surface."

"I am going to be their Sea God. I prefer to have many small islands," Poss countered.

"As the distance between islands is extremely great, many of them will be uninhabited by the human-like creatures. Therefore I ask you, to whom are you going to be the Sea God?"

"Athena is right," Prom said, "at the beginning they are going to be very primitive. Even if there are only a few populated islands, I would be concerned about their health. They cannot interact with others to exchange medical information. I want them to know how to use medicinal plans and how to create medicines. On a mega-continent, they can easily exchange this kind of information with each other."

Athena stopped directly in front of Arr.

He continued to say nothing. Gazing at him she said, "Arr, you and I are warriors. There are going to be tribes on a mega-continent. There will be fighting. Watching then from our ship will be wonderful entertainment. With nothing but very distant little islands, warfare will hardly be possible. And we know as soon as they reach a certain level of civilization, we have to turn our ship around and leave. We don't want to be detected by their sensors."

Arr smiled widely at her.

"But I am in favor of the mega-continent. What makes you to think I am not?"

Athena turned back to Poss.

"As a warrior yourself, don't you agree that on a mega-continent, we will see more fighting?"

"Yes." Poss said sharply.

"And remember, there will be lots of islands still remaining."

"Okay, okay," Poss said grudgingly, "You convinced me. I'm in favor of a mega-continent too."

"Perfect!" Athena smiled widely around at the others. "We have one single issue left then. We need an expert to implement the planetary modifications required to create the mega-continent," she continued seriously.

All eyes were locked on Heff.

"I can handle it." Heff said with pride.

"I am confident you can," Athena said. "But there will be a great deal of energy and matter consumption involved. Zeu might be not happy with that."

"There will be minimum energy consumption. The tectonic plates are practically flooding in the melted lava. I can generate controlled mega-explosions that will push the plates and cause them to collide together."

"Wonderful!" Athena was excited.

"I don't think I'll even need to use antimatter explosions", Heff said. "Atomics might be strong enough."

Athena smiled widely at him.

"I am sure Discordia will be more than happy to assist you."

"You forgot something," Prom noted to Athena.

"What would that 'something' be?" she retorted bitterly.

"Zeu doesn't want a mega-continent."

Athena started laughing. "There are five of us here in favor of it: Afronda, Herr and Discordia also vote yes. I haven't asked Apoll yet, but I expect no big opposition from his side. Zeu appears to be the only one who is on the no side, for now." Athena looked to the men around her. "As far as I know, we are still a democracy on this matter. It looks like Zeu has no choice."

CHAPTER 10

Politics

Sometimes things go in an unexpected direction, not necessarily in a logical one. And this because of politics.

Zeu, personal journal

Prom was walking up and down in the little amphitheater. 32 pairs of eyes were watching him. They were the youngest people of the ship but already had lived several millennia and were therefore old enough to attend sophisticated presentations. However, their appearance was as teenagers on the ship. Still, it was strange for Prom to admit they had numbers as name and not real names.

He had been lecturing for more than an hour, explaining more theories and supporting them with numbers and images in his holographic projections. The final image of his presentation was showing the planet with a mega continent.

"And this is what we have now," he concluded, proudly showing the hologram.

The huge blue ball was suspended in the air. Its blue was now flawed by a large dark stain.

For several seconds Prom contemplated the huge hologram, expecting his students to do the same. Instead he could hear them murmuring like they were not in agreement. He felt like his one-hour presentation had not convinced them. For a moment he felt a terrible frustrated sensation. He called upon his deep mental training to help him to pass this moment. Finally, he turned to his audience and smiled broadly at them.

The hushed murmuring suddenly stopped as he turned to them.

"I guess you want to make some statements. If so, this is the right time."

"I would like to make one," a student with blond curly hair and blue eyes said. "I am Student Seven. Do not confuse me with brain number seven." The entire audience started laughing.

Prom was smiling widely. He felt student number seven wanted to get the audience on his side. Prom instantly assessed that Seven was going to make a negative statement about his presentation. *But why?* Prom asked himself. He decided to use all of his formidable skill in this confrontation.

"You wasted such a big amount of energy to move the tectonic plates to create this mega continent and…"

"I understood Heff explained to you yesterday the amount of energy was not that large because the explosives were placed in strategic points." Prom interrupted him.

"Sure, sure," Seven nodded. "Up to a point I agree with your theory."

"Up to a point?" Prom queried.

"Yes! In creating a mega continent, you are creating a single planetary experience," a blond-haired blue-eyed girl said. She looked like she was Seven's sister. "I am Student 27," she said.

"27, I disagree with what you are saying," Prom gazed her, then moved his eyes to Seven as if to say - *I disagree with you too*.

"There is to be a single continent. Its name is Pangee. Afronda proposed this name in the memory of Gee. There will be a single mega continent indeed, but it is quite large for a primitive civilization. Evolution will occur differently in Pangee's various geographic locations. There will be many tribes first, and many countries after. We are going to see a fascinating live show. I assure you."

"No doubt," a very muscular guy with dark skin and hair said. "But if there would be two distant mega continents, it will be like you are watching two planets. I am Student 32 by the way."

"But the amount of energy ..." Prom tried to protest.

Flashing a grin around the room, number 27 said, "You just told us, due to controlled explosions it is easy to move the tectonic plates that are floating in the melted core lava of the planet."

"True," Prom said. "But as I mentioned in my presentation I care about how the medical information will be transmitted. I want the information to flow easily across Pangee. If there are two mega continents there will be a minimum of two very different worlds. I wouldn't put too much attention on this." For a few seconds there was silence in the room.

"Also, Zeu doesn't want to change too many things on

the planet. Convincing him to add together the volcanic islands and to create Pangee was a massive undertaking already," Prom was trying to be very convincing.

"Sorry .... I am number Thirteen." Complete silence fell upon the room. Usually when he said something the other students paid very close attention.

Prom gazed at Thirteen. *What's so spectacular with this student?* Prom asked himself. *Compared to other students who were looking nice and young, this one was looked rather old.* Prom was trying to find a single word to describe this student. *Yes. He looked old.* Thirteen had a nice body but it was far more mature than the others. Not to mention the long hair and beard, but so white - like the color given by aging.

"We might have more debate about the advantage of having two mega continents," Student Thirteen was suggesting.

"We can discuss this further. Of course, I am open to pro- and counter arguments. Does anyone in the room have any counter arguments about having two mega continents?" Prom asked, casting his gaze around the room and hoping to have a few allies on his side. But there were none.

"Yes, Student Number Thirteen," Dem said to him with a friendly smile. Hest smiled at him too. "Why do you think we need three continents?"

The room was totally white. Amazing technology made it impossible to see the line of the walls. It was as if they were in the middle of nowhere, in a white universe. The two ladies were dressed in flowing white dresses and they were sitting in white chairs. The chairs were very sophisticated with tall backrests. Thirteen was standing in front of them. He was dressed in a long white robe too. His white hair and beard made him appear like he was a part of the white universe created by the white room.

"It would be easier if you allowed me to come prepared with a holographic presentation," Thirteen smiled nicely at the two ladies.

"That won't be necessary," Dem continued smiling at him. "We know you have skills in preparing holographic presentation though and we are very proud of your abilities."

"You are too kind Ma'am." Student Number Thirteen dipped his head.

"Your words will be enough here," Hest finished for Dem.

"I am suggesting a continent a bit different than the other two that have almost been agreed upon. This one will be a small continent."

"An island then," Dem tried to conclude.

"Not exactly," Thirteen answered. "It would be too large to be considered an island. The project is to have the principal mega continent called Eurrass divided into three continents. The passage between Eurr and Affra is going to be quite narrow, separated by a small sea. However, the sea will be large enough to be an obstacle for the first primitive humans to cross from Eurr to Affra. Eurr and Assa are going to be separated by mountains. Otherwise, Affra will have a little shore passage to communicate with Assa. The three parts of Eurrass will be somehow separated."

"We agreed already." Dem said in an important voice.

"The newly created Amerr is going to be a longer

continent spread in both hemispheres of the planet. We can call south Amerr and north Amerr. In the middle there will be a narrow passage between them. This continent is designed like a second alternative of the planet. Our experiments will be quite redundant," Thirteen paused, trying to smile at the two ladies.

He is not accustomed to smiling, Hest instantly thought. She tried to fill her mind with childhood memories and not focus too much on thinking about Thirteen. *It is highly suspected that he can read minds due to his natural abilities. That's why brain number seven is monitoring him so closely.*

With a suspenseful moment created, Thirteen continued. "Also, this continent, mainly South Amerr is going to be used for some secret purposes. Secret for the later humans that will be the inhabitants of the planet."

"You are referring to...?" Dem questioned.

"I am referring to mining the planet, building some pyramids for observation and so on."

"Very well Thirteen. All looked good until now," Hest said approvingly. "Why a third one then?"

"I already said it will be too big to be considered an island. It will be situated in the southern hemisphere in a very good climate. No winter there."

"Lovely," Hest admitted. "But you didn't make your point very clear. Why would we need this little continent?"

"For you ladies."

"Oh..." Dem and Hest were looking at each other. "That is interesting." Dem and Hest were smiling at him.

"I am sure you want to have a continent for only you ladies. You might be able to prove to Herr that your genetic research is more advanced. You can create different looking animals, compared to other continents, and so on."

"And, you might what - assist us with even top-secret research experiments?" Hest tried to make him to confess.

Thirteen admitted this by bowing his head.

"Thanks for coming up with this proposal Thirteen," Dem said.

"We approve it," Hest said.

"But, we don't want this to appear like a demand from us to Zeu and the teams," Dem said, convinced.

"It should appear like…" Hest appeared to look for the right word, "an accident."

This time Thirteen appeared to be a little bit confused. "What exactly are you proposing, ladies?"

"You go to work with Heff on modeling the new approved continents. When you are placing the explosive devices, arrange them in a way that the new little continent is created by a secondary effect of dislocating Amerr from Eurrass, apparently."

"I am confident I can make this happen exactly as you just described, Ma'am."

"Perfect! We are so pleased for the private assistance you are providing us. Good job!"

"Thank you, Ma'am."

"We are settled then."

"Yes Ma'am," he tried to smile. "I hope this will melt the ice between us." Bowing, he then turned and left the room.

For a moment Dem and Hest looked at the place where Thirteen had been standing. "What was that about ice?"

CHAPTER 11

The ice planet

Sex is an important factor in love.

Apoll, The official journal

"Ice, ice, ice!" Herr was so infuriated. "I can't believe you have played so irresponsibly with the planet!" She looked angrily at Zeu. She was wearing a very fashionable dress which showed off her lovely form.

"Silence woman!" Zeu screamed. He was dressed in a skin tight black outfit. Due to a cool video effect, they appeared to be out in space. Only the planet was the nearby cosmic object; nothing else was around. Also, the empty space had an enjoyable echo. The echo was still reverberating in the space for several long seconds after Zeu screamed.

Poss Heff and Afronda were several steps from Zeu and Herr. It was supposed to be a very restricted meeting. Poss and Heff had been actively involved in the last planet project. Also, Afronda was allowed to be present too. In a stylish dress, she was looking at the planet pretending to ignore the harsh dialog between Herr and Zeu.

"I hope you don't think you scare me with your pathetic screaming," Herr said angrily. She stepped closer to Zeu. "Look at the planet and see the effects of your irresponsible actions!"

Instead of looking at the planet Zeu pushed Herr, who stumbled back and almost fell down. "I don't allow you to criticize me! Especially when you were among the group who forced me to approve the creation of a mega continent and split it in two after."

Herr protested loudly, "Not even into two, in three. I don't blame you for that actually. I blame you for this side effect. The split of the continent should be done in a responsible manner. Do you see what we have now?" Finally she screamed: "A ball of ice!"

"Hmm..." Zeu tried to calm himself down.

"You know the split into two continents was approved by Dem and Hest," Zeu appeared for a moment to be making an effort to avoid a confrontation with Herr.

"And you ugly man," Herr turned to Heff. "You think you are brilliant, but in fact you are not able to calculate some simple tectonic plate movements."

Heff smiled at Herr. At least as much as he was able to smile nicely. "I understand you are mad Herr, but this is not because of my explosions. My little toys, as I called them," he seemed faintly amused. "The absorption of the carbon dioxide was the reason. Actually, I thought the planet was going to be quite hot under the greenhouse gas effect. I calculated exactly the amount of carbon dioxide that would be released due to the volcanos I started." He moved his eyes to Poss. Poss was wearing almost the same skin tight black outfit as Zeu. Initially, he had no intention of participating in the discussion.

Finally, Poss decided to start his explanations, "It was nearly impossible to predict this. I knew the rocks had some capability to absorb the carbon dioxide and create carbonates, but it was hard to estimate the scale. The carbon dioxide was supposed to stay contained in the atmosphere and create the greenhouse gas effect."

"How you were so naïve as to not calculate the effect of rains? They carried the carbon dioxide toward the absorbent rocks." Herr said in a wondering voice.

"Heff didn't tell me much about the rocks and the fact they are so carbon dioxide absorbent."

Heff was angry now. He said in a low voice: "You solely collected your own samples, tested them and ran your own simulations. Do not blame me for this."

"The computer simulation suggested some absorption. I can see now the scale was wrongly estimated." Poss tried to defend himself.

"Wrongly estimated!" Herr almost screamed, "Without carbon dioxide and its greenhouse gas effect the planet became frozen. And it will be like this for billions of years. We need to finish this stage at once."

"But it is beautiful," Afronda said.

"Don't start that again Afronda! The surface is at least minus sixty degrees C units. How can this be beautiful?"

"Look at it," Afronda said. "So white and such a perfect sphere. To me, it is an image of beauty."

"Maybe," Herr said ironically. "But we need the ice ball

to become the blue planet again. That blue we waited for such a long time."

"Herr, you know we can wait. We are immortal. Time is irrelevant," Afronda persisted with her arguments.

"Yes. But we have waited too long already. Almost nineteen billion years."

"Why are you so concerned?" Zeu asked.

Herr was turned toward him as if suggesting: *I don't believe you are asking me such a senseless question.*

"Because…, we don't know if life was preserved down there for such a long period of winter."

"Of course it was," Afronda said in a peaceful voice. "I understand our monitoring instruments were destroyed or gravely affected during the freezing process, but the most reasonable assumption is that the life was preserved. You know this too Herr. You are just too upset right now."

"Maybe Afronda is right," Zeu said. "But I also agree with Herr, maybe we have already waited too much. I think we have to wake up the planet," he paused to check faces of the other leaders around the room.

"What can we do now?" Herr asked meditatively "as the planet is an ice ball all the solar radiation is virtually non-existent as they are reflected out. At this point we are not confident if life is surviving under the ice down there. We need to send some devices to check for this. Poss, you should run some simulations to determine what the right chemistry would be to wake up the planet."

"I already did it. The answer is easy. More carbon dioxide."

"What?" Herr wondered.

"Yes. It is going to create the greenhouse gas effect. It

will heat up the planet, melt the ice and soon we will have the blue planet back." There was silence for a few moments.

"But the carbon dioxide might be absorbed again by the rocks!" Herr exclaimed.

"No," Poss said firmly." The rocks are quite saturated with the carbon dioxide. There are enough carbonates within the planet now."

"And from where can we take this amount of carbon dioxide?" Afronda asked.

"Heff can create volcanos at a planetary scale. They will generate carbon dioxide."

"I agree!" Herr said happily. "But, please make a better estimate this time. We still need some carbon dioxide to stabilize the absorbent rocks, some to generate the greenhouse effect and to heat the planet. Otherwise, no more and no less carbon dioxide! We need the right quantity," she looked first to Poss and Heff and finally she gazed at Zeu.

"Fine," Zeu said. "Heff, it looks like you have to send your tools down there again to generate mega explosions and start volcanos. I am sure Discordia is anxious to help you." He paused for a few moments, "As Herr said, no mistakes this time!"

Discordia was having a telepathic dialog with brain number seven.

"Why are you so much in love with that frozen planet?"

"Because of you."

"Of me?" Discordia stood began walking to the middle of the control room. John and Emm didn't turn to her, but they were watching her in a little survey screen. They were concerned about the nervousness of their leader as they weren't aware of her telepathic communications.

Discordia was dressed in a white spandex dress, fitted very tightly to her tall body. It appeared like her dress was a part of the white planet. She stepped briskly, beating the control room's floor with the click-clacking of her heels.

"Why because of me?" She sent her telepathic thoughts to brain number seven.

"Once... I used to love you, it consumed me like the heat of a thousand suns. Now I am more comfortable loving something cold, like this ball of ice. Like this ice planet."

"I can't believe you abandoned me!" Discordia stopped in the middle of the control room. "You abandoned me first. Remember?"

"Well...the circumstances were a bit difficult at that time. I was thinking about a little break, nothing more."

"I understand."

Brain number seven was silent for a few moments, "Now, please, let me love this ice planet."

Discordia started her walk again. "Don't be a loser. We are going to wake up the planet soon. I just prepared the huge atomic explosives for Heff. He will inject them into the earth and the explosions will start volcanos at a planetary scale. You will be again without a love interest."

"I know..." despite the telepathic conversation Discordia distinguished sadness in brain seven's communication. He continued, "Some universes exist only in our minds."

CHAPTER 12

Explosion

Beauty comes with terrible extinctions.

Afronda, Team discussions

Athena, Afronda and Poss were watching the planet through a large window.

"I prefer the direct view instead of holographic projections," Athena said.

Afronda and Poss only nodded. They were focused on watching the planet.

"The planet is waking up," Afronda said.

"Yes." Poss agreed. "Heff sent his big toys deep down again and he started the volcanos at a planetary scale. There is heat from volcanos, but in fact the carbon dioxide will create the greenhouse gas effect and solar radiation is going to be trapped and..."

"Yes, yes we know the details," Athena interrupted him abruptly. "How about ozone?"

"Ozone?" Poss wondered.

"We want ozone Poss," Afronda said in a sexy voice. "And you can't refuse us." She went close to him, touching his arm with a sensual gesture.

"Of course, this oxygen molecule with triple oxygen atoms is efficient to filter the solar radiation..." but Poss was not able to finish as Athena interrupted him again.

"We want the planet better protected against dangerous solar radiation."

"I am not sure that I am authorized to make some changes at a planetary scale. So...I don't understand what you expect me to do?" Poss wondered.

"Apoll is with an auxiliary ship near this system's sun," Afronda said. "As Heff is modifying this planet with his devices, Apoll is influencing the Sun. Also, he is charging our energy devices from the sun's nuclear reactions, harvesting some helium for us and so on. But here..."

"We want ozone," Athena completed for Afronda. "Arr is with other auxiliary ship near Marr planet. I can't believe he has a kind of life there too," Afronda said. "However, I particularly asked Apoll to manipulate the sun in a certain way," she paused, gazing at Poss.

"We sent some data to your private computer," Athena said. "We need you to run a particular simulation."

Poss felt unable to speak. He understood this had to be done in secret and Zeu, Herr, Dem and Hest could not know about it. "Why should I help you out with this? If they find out, we are dead."

"It is not a big deal," Athena said. "This is only a simulation. Not a criminal act. Don't get so scared."

Poss started to breathe normally. "What about the simulation?"

"These particular solar radiations might create a water hydrolysis process," Afronda said. "Therefore, some oxygen will be produced. We need you to estimate how this will change the oxygen balance in the planet overall and how much ozone could be generated," Athena gave Poss a huge smile.

"If you know the planet's chemistry at such a detailed level, why you not run this simulation by yourself?" Poss appeared somewhat offended.

With a sexy walk Afronda stepped closer to Poss, "We did it already. But, you are our main chemist and we trust you very much. We want you to confirm our calculations."

"Explosion!" Herr said in a very loud voice. She was looking around as if checking the effect of this single word on the leaders presented in the room, "This is the correct word."

The leaders were dressed very stylishly, all seated in large and comfortable white chairs arranged in a semi-circle in the middle of the white room. Due to the non-wall effect they appeared like they were sitting in a middle of a white universe. Only Herr was standing up in front, eager to deliver her presentation. She was dressed in a white dress that appeared to be made of squares. Just mathematical lines and right angles. *Science combined with a little fashion. The science creates fashion in fact*, was what she tried to communicate to the audience.

"The explosion of life," she gazed with superiority at the

leaders' group. "Due to the correct amount of oxygen the aquatic life is developing nicely," she smiled happily along the row of leaders.

"Let's start our trip in the planet's life world," she said in an encouraging voice. "I figured out there is an amount of mono cellular life, so far. Here," behind her a holographic projection of a table appeared. First with empty rows and columns, but it started populating as Herr was continuing to speak.

"In the table I added the life forms in the order of their time apparition." The table started to populate with a staggering speed. "You have also a picture of each individual, its order number, scientific name, commonly recommended name and summary description. Also, I added links where you can find the detailed description of each item, and finally, the last column of the table is about its implication in the trophic chain. Now I converted the table in this chart," a chart was replacing the table. "Here, you can shrink the branches of similar individuals in classes of organisms. As a result, the chart will collapse and this might be a user-friendly form where I suggest you use when you perform your own calculations."

The leaders were curiously studying the large amount of data presented in Herr's chart. Herr was moving her eyes randomly over the people in the room. Additionally, her computers were studying the facial expression of each member and giving her immediate feedback. She knew if Athena wrinkled her forehead up, it would be better to come up with more details on the currently explained topic. If Poss started playing with his fingers, he didn't agree with the current sentence and she had better come up with the right arguments to convince him before he spoke up. And so on. Studying facial expressions was allowed, but the psychological examination of leaders' minds was forbidden by Dem and Hest. *They don't want us to get knowledge on this technique,* Herr couldn't stop a fugitive thought.

However, the feedback from her computers was good enough for her to adjust the speech accordingly and make all the leaders present in the room happy.

As usual, Afronda was a master in disguising her thoughts. Her intimate thoughts were nearly impossible to be read or guessed at.

"Why are you almost always using two words for the scientific name?" Afronda asked.

"Because, this is science and these are the names recommended from our original planets. I tried to come up with names as close as possible when the organisms are very similar."

"But they are mono cellular form of life, even a number was going to be enough," Afronda persisted.

"Firstly, I consider them to be the very foundation of life. I highly respect them. That's why I decided to assign two words for their scientific name. I get your point Afronda. Secondly, they have order numbers in the chart, these are the numbers you are referring to. If it is easier for you, just use their order numbers. But, please, accept that there is no reason to spend much energy to change all their names," Herr paused as if waiting for Afronda's permission.

Afronda savored her victory for several moments and finally approved Herr to go on with a slightly perceptible head gesture.

Herr was moving toward the complicated holographic

chart projection, "Now, in this sheet you have microscopically multicellular form of life." A new table sheet appeared behind her and the previous chart sheet disappeared automatically.

"What I would like to highlight in this table are the few flagellates in the position 2327 of the current sheet."

"Now," a new spreadsheet appeared and the old one migrated to the back, "we can see the little algas." The spreadsheet was quite long. "You can see the alga groups here. But, as we have a big variety I used twenty spreadsheets solely for algae. I wanted to get all of them." Herr was kidding with herself.

"They have chlorophyll," Herr paused and addressed the audience with a victorious smile. "The chlorophyll with its 55 carbon atoms - its chemical formula is here - allow them to perform photosynthesis. As you very well know, it is the ability to generate oxygen metabolizing water and carbon dioxide," Herr paused again, looking around the audience. The spreadsheets continued to appear one after the other. The old spreadsheets were migrating into the back as a new one was appearing.

"There is going to be lots of oxygen then," Poss added.

"True," Herr admitted slowly walking at the front. "However, the matter is that I have little aquatic primitive animals that are eating these algas." Several spreadsheets showed up, one after another, showing pictures of little animals, their names and other scientific data.

"I need to play with bigger aquatic animals to keep these little water herbivores under control," Herr was moving back to the hographic projection.

"Personally, I like this trilobite. He is practically cleaning the bottom of the sea. He is eating the death plankton."

"It is like the little robots that are cleaning our ship," Herm observed.

"True," Herr turned to Herm. "However, I don't like this comparison." A little upset, she turned back to her holographic spreadsheet.

"Here we have the biggest life forms." The spreadsheets showed a big variety of strange fish. "This one is a little monster. He is able to chase trilobites even if they have a hard shell."

"Good job Herr," Zeu said.

All the leaders smiled nicely at Herr as they applauded.

Politely Herr smiled back at them. Politely she answered back: "Thank you. I am very happy with our blue aquatic live planet."

A large white large chair materialized behind her. She sat on it, moving her eyes around the room. Finally, she fixed on Herm. There was an uncomfortable moment of silence. Then she asked, "Can you share with the leaders your earliest criticism?"

"Herr…, it was just a private question between you and me," Herm answered back in a defensive but calm voice. "Don't take it personally Herr."

"I don't," she said. It was supposed to be a polite answer but her voice was very cold. "Herm asked me earlier, *why I don't have terrestrial life?*"

As all the leaders remained silent, she continued, "It is true that I don't have terrestrial life. Not yet. But I am going to fix that soon," she accentuated every word. "The sun's radiation is too high. Deadly to these animals and plants. I need there to be more oxygen as when it reaches the superior layer of earth's atmosphere, under the effect of solar radiation, it is converted to ozone. There was an ice hydrolysis process," her eyes moved to Athena and Afronda, "But, unfortunately, we still don't have enough ozone."

"What's the plan, Herr?" Discordia asked in her tiny voice. "I am ready to help."

Instead of looking at Discordia, Herr gazed toward Zeu. "I will produce the requested oxygen from carbon dioxide, through algae's photosynthesis. But...I need to kill the aquatic herbivore life forms at a planetary scale."

"How?" Heff asked trying to arrange his deformed body in the chair.

"By multiplying the carnivores at the same scale," Herr smiled kindly to the audience.

CHAPTER 13

Extinction

*Those who create life but then
desire extinction shortly thereafter
have narrow minds.*

Herm, secret journal

Prom and Arr were in the combat room. They had already been fighting for almost an hour. They were dressed in skin tight spandex catsuits, so tight they appeared naked. The battle had been relentless, and they were both drenched in sweat.

Arr tried several lightning-quick attacks but Prom was able to nimbly move to defend them all. Arr moved back several paces as he tried to get his breathing under control.

"You are a good fighter, Prom. My congratulations."

"I think you and all the other leaders underestimated me," Prom replied, also out of breath.

"Yes, it would seem so," Arr conceded.

Arr tried to surprise him again with a quick attack, but Prom fended him off without much difficulty.

"Time for a break," Arr suggested.

Prom smiled and dipped his head in a salute to signal the fight's end. Arr did the same and the two men sat on the floor.

"I still can't believe Herm was questioning Herr so directly," Arr said incredulously.

"I think she is making mistakes; she should pay attention to our suggestions," Prom replied sharply.

"I value the advice that you and others are giving, but Herr and I are not the same person," Arr admitted. "Why don't you come with me to the nearby planet, on Marr to observe the life forms there?"

"I am doing well here. I can watch the life on Marr on the live cameras. I am aware of all the evolution there. However, I am not interested as that planet can't sustainably support life for the long term."

"True," Arr agreed sadly. "I can't believe after such an extended period of time Herr still doesn't have enough oxygen and the ozone layer is not thick enough."

"It will be soon," Prom said calmly. "She has gotten various species of lichens growing already. Soon there will be plants and animals..."

Prom was unable to finish his sentence as a holographic projection appeared without warning in the middle of the room. The two of them jumped up, startled for a moment as neither of them had requested anything from the computers.

Herr's holographic image came into focus, seated in the middle of the room. In a calm voice she announced, "Sorry for the inconvenience but I want all of you to see this."

"What a heck is this?" Arr's gaze swiveled back and forth between the hologram and Prom.

A seaside vista appeared within the hologram and the image zoomed close to the water's surface,

"A fish?" Arr was wondering, "She is interrupting all the activities on the ship to show us a fucking fish?"

Prom was focusing carefully on the three-dimensional holographic projection, staring intently and unblinkingly at the images. Finally, he turned to Arr and said, "A fish, yes. But what she is showing us is a monumental event. This fish is literally the first animal out of the water."

"This fish made history, you mean," Arr said ironically.

Herr was sitting at the end of the table, opposite Zeu. On the top of the table were her spreadsheets, which now included plants and animals. The sheets were appearing in sequence, one after another.

"It is quite some time now since the first animal stepped out of the water," Herr said proudly about the information she was delivering to the elegantly dressed leaders around the table.

"The plants have increased an evolutionary level. They have now evolved from a reproductive method of spores to one of seeds. This is superior because the seeds are able to carry their own food supply. Because of this, they don't depend on a body of water for survival, enabling them to lay dormant for months or even years before sprouting and to move inland before they do so. As we have more plants, they will produce more oxygen. It is beginning to appear like a viable and sustainable environment to me."

As she spoke, Herr looked at the leaders around the table. Immediately she noticed a contemptuous smile on

Afronda's face, which she was making no effort to hide. For the moment, Herr decided she had no recourse but to ignore Afronda.

"As I mentioned earlier, the planet is now teeming with life. It deserves the name of Blue Planet. We have algae, fish and terrestrial plants but also please look at this," a three-dimensional holograph showed a peculiar looking insect flying with a remarkable speed.

"It is similar to a dragonfly," Herm observed. "I like it."

"You may call it a dragonfly if you wish," Herr replied. "Actually, in this spreadsheet you can see its scientific name and other remarks regarding this species. However, it is too large to be a true dragonfly."

"So..." Prom interrupted, "it is a monster."

"Yes," Herr confessed. "Simply put, if you are there on the planet it can kill you in a blink of the eye. However, if you are patient enough you might observe there are even more monsters," she continued with pride and importance in her voice. "They belong to the insect families of species, but regarding their dimensions, they are monsters," Herr smiled cheerfully at the audience.

"This world is full of giants," Zeu observed. "We might want to save their DNA structures. We can use them as weapons on other planets if we want to exterminate the dominant species there."

"I have already saved their DNA," Herr looked at Zeu, "I thought their DNA might be valuable for that purpose as well."

"This one for example," Herr continued, pointing at the holographic projection showing a creature with a long, curved wicked looking tail. "It is a scorpion-like insect. It is six feet long. And," she paused and quickly looked around the audience, "It is a vicious predator."

"Nice..." Arr said in an approving tone.

Herr grinned at him. "Isn't it?" The two of them were enjoying the predator's image.

"Herr, if I understood correctly, all of this is due to an excess of oxygen. Their respiratory systems are more efficient. As a result, they grow bigger. Am I right?" Athena asked.

"That's correct. That makes them grow larger." Herr confirmed. "We even have animals that are reproducing with eggs. Like a seed, an egg contains all the required nutrients, including water. I believe this is a major evolution. As you see, the land is fully occupied by animals. In a long-ago meeting, we said we had a marine life explosion. Now we have a terrestrial life explosion."

"You are referring now to reptiles," Poss remarked.

"Exactly," Herr was beaming radiantly at him and the entire audience.

"Reptiles...what disgusting creatures," Afronda said, horrified.

"You might not like them Afronda, but they play a significant role in the evolutionary chain," Herr paused to allow her thoughts to sink in with the audience. Triumphantly, Herr continued, "We have here giant reptiles. You can see their scientific names in this table. I named them using analogies with the life forms known on our original planets. We have Scutozores, Curozores, and so on. Look at this Ogonoze – it is in fact a killing machine. It hunts Scutozores." The hologram was now showing three-dimensional videos of the creatures Herr had listed chasing, killing, or simply waylaying other animals.

"The Ogonoze is your favorite now," Prom said to Arr, "not the previous gigantic scorpion."

Interrupting their conversation Herr continued, "As I said, the earth is teeming with life." Herr was extremely proud of herself. "I hope you all agree we have a nice wide variety of organic life down there on the planet."

"Nice?" Afronda asked in a very calm voice. She was not even looking to the hologram as she carefully arranged her lovely dress around her, as if she was so preoccupied with her dress she was talking to herself. But her words were addressed to Herr's speech.

"How can you, in any way, use that adjective for what is down there?"

Herr was visibly irritated by Afronda's interjection. "And what other…adjective would you wish me to use?" Herr abruptly crossed her arms over her chest as her voice began to rise. She was standing and gazing down at Afronda irritably.

I like Afronda, Prom was thinking.

Afronda is so unpredictable, Arr was musing simultaneously. *It is so fortunate I didn't have to face her.*

*It is quite foolish of Afronda to challenge Herr. Particularly here and now…*Discordia thought to herself.

"Grotesque. Ugly. Disgusting." Afronda said, pausing between each word and punctuating them in a tone designed to offend Herr even more. "Those are adjectives you should use." Now she looked at Herr defiantly. "I understand we each have a different perception of beauty. But my definition is the correct one." Afronda's voice was crystal clear.

The two women stared at each other for several moments, silently feuding.

Finally, Afronda turned to Zeu. "My mandate here is to correct all of you when you waver from the proper definition of beauty. None of you can stop me from fulfilling my duty. Not Gee, not Herr, and certainly not you!" She declared as she glared at him.

Pausing to look around the room, she continued sharply, "I demand that the current organic life on this planet be eradicated as soon as possible."

A long cold silence followed her statement.

Slowly, Herr sat down on her chair by the table. It was clear that she was making a huge effort to control herself and keep her voice calm. "If these creatures are not as beautiful as you wish, what do you want then Afronda? A mass extinction?"

"Yes," Afronda answered. "An extinction at a planetary scale." She went back to artfully arranging her dress again.

"Only because they are not beautiful in your eyes, you want to kill...all of them? To make them extinct?" Herr asked. This time her voice was shaking.

"Do not take this personally, Herr. But down there is not at all the world we came here to see or create," Afronda declared.

"I understand this," Herr stood up and walked around the table as if trying to gain sympathy from the leaders seated around the table. "But...extinction. We may be able to find alternative ways."

"None would be quick enough compared to the extinction," Zeu added. He and Afronda were nodding at each other in agreement.

"I appreciate your great power of understanding, Zeu," Afronda batted her eyes at Zeu. "Actually, I am impressed." Finally, she directed an unfriendly look towards Herr.

"I am against the Extinction," Arr said in with an irritated voice. "We need to consider this deeply and then have a vote."

"There will be no vote," Zeu said loudly.

Arr was about to say something in reply but when he met Zeu's cold eyes he didn't dare to speak.

"As you know Discordia's proposal to have a secondary mega continent was approved but not yet completed. Dem and Hest request that be done soon. I had held off temporarily but now is an appropriate time as we are not satisfied with the current organic life on the planet. Heff, prepare your under-surface explosives to split and move the continent. I am sure Discordia would be more than happy to assist you."

Discordia smiled politely at Zeu, who continued. "Also, a few students of Dem and Hest might be interested in assisting you with this."

"I will make the arrangements immediately," Heff said, as he avoided looking in Herr's direction.

Zeu turned to Herr, "I won't call this process extinction. I will call it the split of the secondary continent."

"But due to toxic gases from planetary volcanos, 99% of the earth 's life is going to die." Poss asserted.

"So what?" Afronda's voice was increasing in volume. "It is ugly organic life."

Herr walked back to her chair. She looked at Zeu and murmured quietly, "I understand we have to do this. I am going to call it the Permian Extinction."

CHAPTER 14

Dinosaurs

They criticize me because I create monsters. But as the herbivores are reproducing at such a large scale they are affecting the vegetation at a planetary scale. Therefore, the oxygen balance is affected at the same levels and this simply cannot be allowed to happen. Please understand, I need monsters!

Herr, Teaching the young students

"There is a massive extinction down there," Hest said.

"Yes, the Permian Extinction. The toxic volcanic gases killed effectively all life on the planet," Dem agreed.

The two ladies were dressed comfortably in loose dresses. They were seated at a little table near a large circular window facing the planet. They were consuming hot drinks from large delicate cups.

"I prefer the direct view of the planet," Dem sipped from her cup.

"Yes, it appears much more...alive compared to holograms."

"Also, it is not very cloudy today; that's why we have this lovely view."

"Yes. We can see the continent."

"But also, a large shift in the continents."

"Yes. The second mega continent can now be seen. Even the third smaller one."

"Our continent."

"Yes."

"They are not very distant yet."

"For now."

"They have already named the second mega continent Ammer. We should let them know the name of the third one. Zeu asked us to name it as a courtesy."

"He is a good leader. I like him better than I liked Uran."

"Let's call the continent Ausstra."

"It is a pretty name and in accordance with Ammer, somehow."

"Our students did an excellent job."

"Especially...him."

"He and the other students were working with Heff. The formation of the third little continent appeared as a side consequence. Not even Heff is aware of it."

The ladies fell into a short pause as they sipped from their large cups.

"And the first mega continent?"

"Actually, it is going to be composed of three

sub-continents. Eurr, Assa and Affra. Affra is going to remain connected with Assa by a narrow passage, which might stay under water for a while. Eurr will be separated by Assa by a chain of tall mountains."

"Nice. They are going to be somehow separated continents."

"Exactly. When we have human-like beings, it will be interesting to watch them fighting to survive on these continents."

Hest and Dem looked down at the planet admiring the view.

"Life will recover from the volcanic gases soon. I wish the continents were more distant from each other."

"I know. This time the animals and plants might be homogenous everywhere as the continents are still close to each other."

"It might not end up being a very interesting phase then."

"That's why we might need a new extinction at the end of this phase too."

The two ladies smiled at each other conspiratorially.

———◆———

Apoll and Arr had been making love for over an hour. While Arr usually preferred sex in a dark room, Apoll liked a bright one. Arr hated to compromise but the sex was so incredibly hot and sensual he had agreed to leave the lights on. They broke apart, their bodies gleaming and covered in sweat.

"Man, having sex with you is so much better than having sex with your replicas," Arr sighed contentedly.

"Why are you surprised? Any replica of mine is a copy of me and everything was supposed to be copied. However, no replica will ever be able to replace me."

Apoll got out of the bed, walking naked around the room. Standing in the middle of the room he looked down to Arr. "They cannot replace me because I am unique."

"I agree," Arr wanted to argue, but he didn't want to upset Apoll as he intended to have another round of sex.

Apollo sent a mental command to the computer. An enormous hologram appeared in the middle of the room. He started to study it with great attention. "We are almost fifty million years from the Permian Extinction. The planet has begun to heal."

"My love, the planet is quite lifeless right now. Everything is compromised. Animals, plants, all is dead now. And in the ocean, it is the same. The sulphuric acid poisoned everything. Do not waste your energy. Come back to bed. I need you."

Apollo was commanding the computer to show images closer to the land's surface then turned his attention to look down at the ocean. "I can see some species of pink algae. That's why the ocean has a rosy tinge to it. They are able to metabolize the toxic sulphur compounds."

"Yes," Arr was desperately thinking what to say to convince Apoll to come back to bed. "Still it will be millions of years until the ocean's water will be pure enough to sustain fish and other species. Look at my Marr planet. Life is totally extinct there too by now."

"Arr, I am concerned about Terr planet not Marr planet. It was interesting to have two planets sustaining life in the same solar system. But nearly impossible."

"I knew that from the very beginning. I just made a poor parallel between these two planetary situations. Come here, I want to tell you the story of how life disappeared from Marr."

"Can you?" Apoll had some excitement in his voice.

"Yes. Just come here handsome."

"Give me a moment please," Apoll was now surfing through the hologram to the planet's soil. "I can see here small mammals. They were able to survive and evolve because they are able to hide within the earth."

"I can't believe you are paying attention to those stupid rats while I am here naked waiting for you!"

Apollo stopped the hologram and walked back to bed where Arr was waiting for him. He hugged and kissed Arr, "I am back. But, before we make love again, tell me how the life totally disappeared from Marr?"

Zeu was watching with interest the holographic screen full of chemical formulas showed to him by Poss.

"Show me bro," Zeu said to Poss.

"Yes bro. As I said, I am happy with the current gas composition. We have an ozone layer thick enough to protect the planet from deadly solar radiation. The ozone layer was not affected by Sulphur dioxide or other gases."

"This is good. Poss, sometimes, I believe you are the only one here to able to give me good news. The other ones appear to enjoy collecting unwelcome news and delivering it to me." Zeu said with a friendly smile.

"Actually, I have more good news," Poss continued, touching Zeu's shoulder. "Due to the death of all the plants and animals in sea and land, the bubbles of methane are evolving."

"Okay...." Zeu was a little confused as he didn't understand what the good news was here.

"Methane is a greenhouse gas at least twenty times stronger than carbon dioxide. It can push the global temperature up; I estimate it at an average of eleven standard temperature degrees."

"Are you saying it will be hotter than it was before the Permian Extinction?"

"Exactly. All in all, the gas composition is good. The oxygen content is 21.3 percent."

"Right," Zeu became excited. "We are able to breathe down there."

"Correct."

"If there are no other toxic gases to affect us, and the amount of oxygen is at sustainable levels...then why we don't have new species down there on the planet?"

"We do have a few new species of plants and animals down there, and they are going to have a rapid evolution," Poss smiled at Zeu.

Zeu grinned back, "Good bro. Good."

Prom was regretting he was not into guys. He was admiring Poss's naked body. It was a very muscular body; the room was filled with his masculinity. Prom felt in comparison his muscles weren't quite as well developed as Poss's and this made the other man appear more manly. He thought to himself, *If I can adjust my metabolism a little and log more gym time I can have a body almost like Poss.*

Suddenly, Poss turned to Prom. "Are you sure that down there are no deadly viruses or dangerous bacteria?"

"There are some dangerous bacteria but not as many as in the lakes. You are going to swim deep down in the ocean. The saline water has a sterilizing effect in this regard," Prom paused, looking at the young ladies who were helping Poss put on his tight rubber swimming suit. They were all incredibly lovely, Prom wondered how he didn't pay close attention to the crew. *Such beautiful creatures yet he pays no attention to them.* They were wearing tight underwear as they had yet to change into their swimming attire.

"Sir, you don't have to do this," the first one, Zoe, said.

"It appears quite dangerous," Zinca, the second one, added nervously.

"There are still too many bacteria even in the ocean water," the third one Zion, addressed a hostile look at Prom.

"Ha, ha," Prom was laughing back at them. "I already injected you with a vaccine. It is going to protect you if, in a worst-case scenario, you come into contact with these bacteria. The swimming collar is totally isolating you against the external environment. Do not forget Athena is still checking everything. We are not allowed to leave any of our DNA down there, even by mistake. We have to work clean."

Prom sent a mental command to his computers. He asked for three replicas to be made, one for each lady. He intended to have sex with all three of them at once. Their physical presence made him so horny. He was so anxious to go back in his apartment to have some nasty fun.

"However, you should be very, very suspicious about

the water. I mean, you have to pay attention to the water's creatures."

Poss started laughing, "They are just fishes my friend."

"Sir, I can't believe you said that," Zoe said to him. "The earth has changed a lot. We are in fact 50 million years from the Permian Extinction."

"Yes, there are Ethiozores. They are fish, as I said," Poss gave Zoe a hard look as if saying, *do not contradict me.* She fell silent.

"I would say that they are descendants of the reptiles. They were hiding from the Permian Extinction and they evolved here in the water," Prom walked closer to them so they could hear his next words better. "Never trust a reptile."

Poss was looking quite unconvinced.

"It doesn't matter. They are fish now. They are 20 feet longer and can travel almost 20 miles per hour," Zinca added, trying to help Poss.

"It is in fact a type of shark. A fast and ruthless predator," Prom bitterly smiled at Poss's group.

"And they are the first on my list," Poss smiled nicely back at Prom.

"The tentacled species are not that dangerous and they are food for the Ethiozores." Zion pointed out.

"I am familiar with ocean life forms. You guys sent out the related spreadsheets. Usually Herr was doing this job," Prom remarked.

"Correct," Poss agreed. "But for a while now the ocean life is no any longer her business. I guess you missed Zeu's last directive where he specified I oversee the ocean and its life forms."

Poss addressed a critical look to Prom as if saying in a

superior way *I am updated with everything*, then continued, "Also Ethiozores are chased down by Plyosores, and they are my babies," he stated proudly.

"Babies?" Prom wondered.

"They are eight times stronger than an Ethiozores. Plyosores teeth are around 12 inches longer. They can grow up 30 meters longer. A real monster," Prom said seriously. "And a real danger," he continued, "there are threats in the ocean. You had better watch everything from here through our live cams."

Prom was still wondering why Poss seemed so unaware, and he felt like he had to say it. "Sorry Poss, but I think you are ignorant to the danger."

Poss started laughing, "Lucky you. You might have concluded by now it is not only Herr who loves monsters. I love monsters too," he cheerfully admitted.

"And you take all these risks because...?" Prom questioned.

"Because I have an innovative technology that I want to implement myself," Poss replied.

"What about this technology?" Prom was looking at the four people in front of him now dressed in swimsuits as if they were crazy.

"We are aware that many of the babies down there might be lucky enough to swim close to us," Poss said.

"Or try to chase us," Zoe completed for him.

Poss smiled at her. "Yes, but they are going to be thrilled with these little needles."

"Directly in their brains," Zion added.

Prom took a closer look at the minuscule device.

"It is going to create an intimate connection with the neurons in the creatures' brains," Zinca added.

"And why do that?" Prom said, a little confused.

"The little devices are going to send us images from these creatures' eyes."

Instead of being impressed by the explanations around the minuscule devices Prom said sarcastically, "Are you that bored by our live cameras? We have images from everywhere. Secondly, this is a job that can be done perfectly well by our robots."

"You know how much I love the ocean. I won't send a machine to do jobs that I can do myself," Poss said arrogantly.

"Are we at least going to be escorted by our faster fighting robots?"

"We are going to have some protective robots around us," Zoe confirmed.

"Just in case something goes wrong," Zion added.

"Congratulations guys. You have my permission then," Poss said. Then he hurried up to his living quarters, excited to meet the three newly created replicas.

***

The small animal was gazing at them with curious eyes. The leaders were looking down at it. They were in a little amphitheater, the steps of which were also large benches. The leaders were dressed in sexy clothes and they walked around the amphitheater trying to view the creature from different angles.

Downstairs in the amphitheater Herr was delicately touching the lovely baby animal lying there so peacefully.

Herr over fed him, Herm was thinking. *That's why he is so quiet.*

Nearby Herr the little beast was watching the leaders as if trying to memorize their faces.

On the floor of the amphitheater Herr had created a wonderful little garden.

"I have to admit, your garden is lovely, Herr," Afronda approved.

"Thanks!" Herr answered back sarcastically. Her tone was saying: *Thanks, bitch. Would you like a new extinction today? Or tomorrow?*

Athena was attempting to engage in a polite discussion. "I can see such luxuriant vegetation around you Herr. These plants are not from our own collection. Can you please explain?"

"Yes. All are plants from the Terr planet," Herr paused as she looked up into the amphitheater. "We are 100 million years from the Permian Extinction. These plants are all very attractive. Our robots carefully selected them following my explicit instructions. I made sure all of them are compatible with our environment. The trees around me have only several months of growth. When they are mature, they will be gigantic."

"Why are you presenting us with such an extensive vegetation garden but only a single animal?" Herm asked. He was quite fascinated with the small adorable creature.

"Because this is the most successful species on the earth right now," Herr importantly answered. She paused to let the leaders digest the effect of the weighty sentence she had just made. "I call him Dino. He is a baby dinosaur."

"You could have shown us a hologram," Heff observed.

"I feel quite uncomfortable having an animal from the planet here. I know it was carefully scanned but still…"

"No reason to worry Heff. As you can see, I touch Dino. He is a lovely animal," Herr took several moments to pet him gently as he in turn showed enormous pleasure at Herr's every touch.

This dinosaur definitely loves to cuddle, Apoll was thinking.

"I put the descriptions of all the plants and animals online."

"Terrestrial plants and animals you mean," Poss added in a nasty tone.

"Yes," Herr admitted. "Poss and his crew monitor the aquatic life now as it is a large variety there." Herr looked around the amphitheater. Finally, she turned back to Poss.

"Good job by the way."

Poss smiled, happy for this victory.

"But this is an herbivorous animal, Herr," Arr commented. "I thought your favorites are the carnivorous predators."

"True!" Herr said in a lower but convincing voice. She smiled in Arr's direction. "But despite the fact there are few terrestrial predator species, Dino and his relatives are the most dominant species on the planet, so far."

"Remarkable!" Zeu said loudly.

"Thank you, sir," Herr said politely.

The small animal was grazing slowly on some leaves. For a few moments, all the leaders were watching and analyzing the dinosaur. Herr walked through the amphitheater toward Afronda.

"So, when are you proposing the next extinction?" She gazed at Afronda intently.

Dino began coughing as if he understood Herr's words and was concerned about his nearing death.

Herr continued to look at Afronda inquisitively.

"Do not look at me like that Herr," Afronda protested.

Herr was not at all intimidated by Afronda's words. She continued to study Afronda's face.

"My name is Afronda, not *Madam Extinction*!" Afronda said firmly even as she smiled politely back at Herr.

Herr smiled bitterly in return. She turned her gaze to Zeu. "The question still remains."

"Why would we need a new extinction?" Zeu asked Herr.

"This is not a question for me. If you remember, I didn't want the first extinction either."

"A new extinction might be not necessary," Poss said. He looked around at the leaders with a friendly expression on his face. "At least not right now. Let's leave the planet untouched for a while and watch the forms of life evolve."

He appeared as if he was going to say more but as his eyes fell upon Athena's face, he saw her icy expression. He didn't dare to say a word more.

For a few minutes there was silence around the room.

"Watching the planet's evolution without intervention for at least 50 million years is a wonderful idea," Discordia said in her tiny voice. She was looking imploringly at Zeu.

"Ha-ha...." Zeu was laughing. "Let's vote then."

He scrutinized the leaders still scattered around the amphitheater. "Who's for yes?"

CHAPTER 15

The second extinction

Stability often kills evolution.

Athena

Herr and Zeu broke apart, their entire bodies glistening with perspiration. They had been engaged in a marathon sex session. Finally, they decided to take a little break. Herr knew that Zeu need some recovery time. The room had been barely lit with only a few floating electronic candles around the bed. Now, Herr chose the non-wall effect. The walls slowly became transparent and it appeared as if they were right on the planet's surface. Around the bed, dinosaurs walked close by along with predators and other animals. A light breeze could be seen wafting through the nearby vegetation. The room's ventilators and humidifiers were able to reproduce this effect; the cool damp air brushed their bodies. They were near a tropical forest with a huge lake. The humidity filled the room now. Zeu sighed with contentment. Herr was his best friend, practically his wife.

Their long-standing relationship had built complete trust; they never bothered with protected sex now and he pondered why she had not become pregnant.

I know he is wondering why I am not pregnant yet! He might think I took some pills for this, Herr thought to herself. *But this is the result of advanced brain control. I can control my body perfectly, down to the last molecule.* She joked to herself: *it is a matter of identifying the hydrogen.* She tried to teach her young students about this powerful technique. *Once you are able to identify the hydrogen within your body, you can then identify any type of compound.* She knew by now, Zeu was also musing philosophically to himself during this interlude.

"I was absolutely correct," Herr said, proud of herself. "The Dinos are the dominant species. They are so stable. Their DNA looks so beautiful."

"They gave us another 50 million years," Zeu said.

"Unfortunately, those 50 are gone," Herr said in a pensive voice.

"Are they?" Zeu wondered. "Time is flying by. It feels like only yesterday we had our meeting in the amphitheater and agreed to wait at least 50 million years. By the way, you had a wonderful idea to bring in the little Dino at that meeting. That made the leaders more amenable to the idea."

"Yes..." she said, sadly. "Actually, it has been 165 million years since the dinosaurs first appeared. That is three times as long as everyone agreed to. I guess all the leaders love the dinosaurs. Otherwise, I see no explanation."

"I am planning to organize a new meeting to evaluate the status of the planet and decide the next steps," Zeu paused, thinking deeply for a few moments. But he quickly changed his mental direction. "However, I am horny again."

"Let's do it then," Herr said eagerly.

The non-wall effect disappeared. The room become dark again with electronic candles floating around.

With an expert twist of her hips, Herr put Zeu's organ inside her. Zeu was moaning with immense pleasure as they began again. Zeu closed his eyes, intending to enjoy the sexual pleasure to its fullest. Passion hung heavily in the room…then suddenly he opened his eyes and noted with surprise that Athena had entered the room.

With great speed and force he pushed Herr away like she was nothing more than a ragdoll. Herr landed on the floor with a thump crying out in pain, and a trickle of blood in the corner of her mouth from the force of the landing. Zeu's move had been so unexpected and forceful; she had hurt her head badly on the way down.

"How did you get here?" Zeu screamed at Athena.

"I oversee the security of this ship," Athena answered calmly. "Therefore, I can be anywhere at any time I wish."

"But I had the computer lock the door in personal security mode. Nothing should be able to break my passwords!" Zeu was still raging.

"Yet I am standing here," Athena said not impressed at all. "Take it as a fact."

Herr stood up. She hadn't wiped the blood off her face.

They all say this woman loves blood, Athena thought to herself. *Herr is covered with it! I am fortunate I never faced her in a real fight.*

"It is said that Zeu is your father," Herr said to Athena, calmly and quietly. She stood proudly, not at all ashamed to be standing naked in front of Athena. "Your DNA comes from him," Herr was addressing a strange smile toward

Athena. It was as if despite the present situation, Athena was the one in difficulty.

This woman is a bitch. Athena thought sharply.

"How do you know this? The usage of the DNA data base is top secret," Zeu wondered.

But Herr ignored his question as she prepared to deliver a strong lesson to Athena.

"As a good daughter, you should wait until your father was finished with his private affairs. You should show some patience."

"I have been patient an additional 115 million years. We agreed to only 50. In total, I have been waiting for 165 million," Athena answered abruptly. "I am the very definition of patience, whether you agree or not."

"Okay, okay...." Zeu tried to calm the two ladies down. "Why are you here Athena?"

"She is here to ask you for the second extinction. What else?" Herr said with contempt.

"True," Athena admitted. "I already sent you all the data. Just check your computer."

"Why do you want to kill my dinosaurs?" Herr asked, frustrated.

"Because they are a closed evolutionary branch. They have not evolved beyond this stage. I want intelligent human-like beings on this planet as soon as possible."

Athena walked toward Herr. In stark comparison to Herr's proud stance, Zeu was discreetly trying to cover his body.

Athena continued, "You know as well as I do Herr, we have delivered only the first stage of our experiment so far. We created life from inorganic matter. Now we must create true intelligent life. We are not allowed to fabricate it in our laboratories, but we can take action on the planet with as many variables as we need to direct the evolution in a way that will generate intelligent life."

"And what methods are you proposing now? The toxic volcanic gases might not be the best idea. They might totally poison the planet this time," Zeu interjected.

"I have sent all the calculations in a spreadsheet," Athena replied. "We need a planetary winter. Dinosaurs and other reptiles are going to die. However, some mammals will survive. As a result, more intelligent creatures will have a chance to evolve."

"Okay," Zeu admitted. "It seems like a reasonable plan. I am going to organize a meeting with all the leaders tomorrow and you can present this proposal."

"I will explain nothing at the leaders' meeting!" Athena said sharply. "You are going to perform all these actions as it is all your own idea." Athena turned to Herr, "And you are going to stand in silent approval."

"But there is going to be an extinction," Zeu tried to argue. "Why are you so afraid to propose such an important action if that is what you want?"

"Why do they always have to think that I am the bad girl?" Athena smiled sweetly at him.

Confused, Zeu did not reply.

"As Herr said, according to the DNA results you are my biological father. Therefore, you can do something for me," she continued in a sugary sweet tone.

"I would say also for these new so-called intelligent creatures," Herr said disdainfully, "It will be a million years until their appearance and…" it was as if she was forcing herself to be polite, "I hate them already! Such monstrous extinctions for their benefit only."

Athena stepped closer to Herr. "I understand. However, we have to do what we have to do. If it makes it easier for you, consider that this was the natural evolution of your own kind after all."

———◆———

Zeu, Poss, Heff and Herm were in the party room drinking heavily. The holograms created a tavern around them. A few flames in the corners were fighting a losing battle with the darkness. The atmosphere was dim. In the middle of the tavern was a rustic old wooden table. The four chairs around the table echoed the table's rough craftsmanship. Herm had already asked why this odd choice of venue. But, Heff answered back *'to make you to drink more'*. All the group was laughing and drinking heavily.

By now the four of them were quite drunk. They were dressed in old-style masculine clothes which reeked of alcohol due to having been spilt on over and over by unsteady hands. The ventilation software was set up to work according to the chosen scenario and the smell of spilled drink was floating all around. Poss observed that Heff appeared to be the party animal of their immortal life.

Suddenly, Herm was advised by his team that something important might be about to happen. He desperately tried to fight off the alcohol's effects and keep a clear head.

"Guys, is there going to be anything besides this heavy drinking? Wasn't there supposed to be a discussion here too?" Herm asked.

"Yes, yes there might be," Zeu answered, slurring his

words. "But we are not done with the drinking yet. And you Herm, are drinking very slowly."

Herm wondered, "Why did you invite only us? Why not other leaders too?"

"Drinking is not to a lady's taste," Zeu answered back, making a face at Poss and Heff and they all began laughing.

"Other guys then?" Herm was still insisting.

"Apollo and Arr are very busy with their love story," Heff said as he winked at Herm.

"It is a very nice love story indeed," Herm said, trying to put his addled brain in order. He noticed the telepathic connection with his computers was working properly despite the alcohol as he mentally read a note sent by his team members: *ask about Prom.*

"And Prom? Where is he?"

"Well..." Poss began, as he paused to take a sip from his glass. "He is in love with me. Unfortunately, he is still unsure. So... I am waiting."

Sadly, Zeu, Heff and Poss broke out into hysterical laughter. Herm was the only one who did not join in.

He felt nervous for a moment. He sent back a mental command to his computers to make more projections and to figure out what was happening. Finally, he received a message. Due to the alcohol, he wasn't able to gauge whether it was his own thoughts, information from the computer or his team: *ask what you can do to help with the second extinction.*

For a moment Herm was terrified. *This is unbelievable!* He was frantically thinking.

But as the other three were laughing like crazy drunken idiots, he decided to try it.

"What can I do to help you with the second extinction?"

The three men abruptly stopped laughing and became serious, gazing at Herm.

Poss began, "my bro Zeu indeed requires a second extinction. I told him you are the right leader to help."

"Nice," Herm smiled around the table, enjoying a small victory.

"I thought Heff was the master of starting an extinction from the underground."

"True," Heff agreed. "But there are some… problems…" he tried to watch his words carefully as his brain was working slowly with all the alcohol. "I am afraid of some secondary reactions. That's why I recommend not to use the previous extinction method again."

"Also," Poss continued, "Dem and Hest like the current continent disposal plan. Changing it requires lots of data to convince them of the opposite. Therefore, it is better not to even try."

"The planet is very stable," Zeu finally said. "It appears as if nothing on the planet can destabilize it."

"I understand," Herm said in a grave tone. "You want me to look outside of the earth."

"Kinda," Zeu said, taking another long drink from his glass. "I am sending you a report right now."

Instantly Herm was able to read it. Even though it was very long and detailed, he was able to immediately summarize it. It was about a nearby huge asteroid.

"First of all, congratulations Zeu. Well done," Herm nodded approvingly at Zeu.

"Second, I am aware of this asteroid. I will be able to change its path and direct it to collide with the earth in a brief period of time. You are also very correct in your report that this will create an induced winter. That is what you need to kill the dinosaurs."

"Nice," Zeu said simply. "When can you begin work to change the path of this asteroid?"

"My deflecting asteroid technology," Herm paused for a moment, embarrassed. Due to so much alcohol he said *my* when he should have used *our*, "Our... deflecting asteroid technology is impressive, even if we are dealing with a large one, as in this case. It is 30 kilometers in diameter."

"No problem," Zeu appeared quite anxious. "When can you begin?"

"Immediately after this is voted on and approved in the leaders' meeting."

"We are for," Poss said. He started laughing heartily, as if he had just heard a good joke.

"Yes, we are for," Heff approved too.

"No, no.... I am referring to all of the leaders."

Abruptly, Zeu banged the table hard with his fist. The glasses rattled due to the strong vibration.

"I am the Supreme Leader! And you had better do what I say!" He screamed at Herm.

"We are a democracy here...." Herm tried to protest.

"This is not a matter of democracy! This is a technical issue! I must change a stable planet to foster evolution. The study I sent you calculated that we might have intelligent beings soon after these new variables were applied."

He paused to give Herm time to recover, then continued, "Check all the internal regulations. I have the authority to command this. Clear?"

Zeu gazed intently at Herm.

Without hesitation, Herm answered, "Yes sir. You are crystal clear. I won't disappoint you. But just to let you know, there is a chemical problem," Herm addressed Zeu with a serious look.

"Yes?" Zeu wondered. He leaned back on the wooden chair trying to achieve a more comfortable position.

"Iridium," Herm replied.

Zeu, Poss and Heff all wore the same expression, perplexed, they didn't understand.

"That asteroid appears on my maps as one with high iridium content," Heff specified.

"So what?" Poss queried.

"When the planet is finally populated with intelligent creatures, at a certain stage of their evolution, they might be able to understand that the death of the dinosaurs was created by an asteroid that collided with their planet."

"Yes. But it is possible that asteroids might hit the planet randomly. They can't say it was deflected by us from its original path to hit their planet," Zeu said convincingly. "Therefore, we have no problem."

Dem and Hest were seated in comfortable chairs around a little table by their favorite large circular window. They were drinking tea from delicate porcelain cups.

"So...," Dem said, looking at Hest philosophically. "We are going to assist in a rarely seen phenomenon. And we are going to watch it live."

Hest smiled at Dem, "Exactly dear Dem. How is your tea?"

"It is perfect!"

"I instructed Zeu to watch Herm closely when he is moving the ship. The movement of the ship needs to be very smooth because we are having our tea at this time. I don't want any unexpected vibrations."

"He will. He is a good leader. As per protocol, he didn't have to inform us officially about all this. But he informed us as a courtesy."

"Yes. His report is very well done."

"He mentioned that his daughter Athena was the originator of the report," Hest smiled sadly at Dem.

"I don't have any issues with this bit of... nepotism here. Do you?"

Hest appeared to forget to answer Dem's question as she became excited about the live events occurring outside. "Look, the ship is finally moving. Millennia have passed since this ship was moved from its stationary orbit."

"Yes. I was asking myself if Heff 's maintenance team were still checking the main engines as scheduled."

"Of course they are!"

"Just joking, dear."

For a few moments Dem and Hest fell silent as they sipped from their tiny cups. They were watching the planet as the ship moved slowly.

"We need to reposition further from the planet."

"Yes. There is will be lots of debris around the planet. We don't want to get hit accidentally."

They felt the ship stop its movement.

"Look!" Hest said excitedly, "It is coming!"

"Oh... this asteroid is huge. I didn't pay much attention to the numbers."

Mentally using the computer link, Dem opened the report, "It is 30 kilometers in diameter."

"That is large indeed for this purpose. Its dimensions are comparable to the biggest mountain on the planet."

"Yes. Or the newer mountains formed when the Indd continental plate collided with Assa continental plate recently - now we have the Evvr mountains."

"Look the asteroid is approaching."

"Now we have the best view."

"I am sure Afronda finds it… ugly." The two ladies giggled together.

"It is moving so rapidly!"

A shadow seemed to fall upon the giant window, which became darker but still remained transparent.

"This is to protect us. Due to friction with the planet's atmosphere, most of the asteroid will burst into flames and a large part of it instantly vaporized."

Dem and Hest were watching the devastating impact.

"It looks like a bomb exploding."

"Yes. Would you like more tea dear?"

"Yes, please."

"A huge proportion of the vegetation and animals are going to burn."

"Yes. The vegetation will ignite due to the immense heat."

"Imagine how forceful the earthquakes and tsunamis are down there. We will be able to review the video records from the planet. Many of the cameras will be destroyed but some will survive as they have anti-gravitational suspensions and excellent mechanical and thermal protection."

"As per the report, the effects that follow the collision will complete the extinction. This is only the beginning."

"Yes. The debris will block the solar light. The remaining vegetation will then die."

"Without vegetation the Dinos are going to die also."

"Yes. We have been watching them for almost 165 million years. Quite boring..."

"Indeed. Athena's report is quite optimistic. She estimated we might have humans in less than 60 million terrestrial years."

"Quite exciting! Isn't it?"

CHAPTER 16

Evolution

At last the most skilled predators will dominate the planet. It is a rule of evolution. The real fact is, humans are the dreadful predators.

Arr, Lesson to the young students

"40 million years have passed since the second major extinction," Herr said.

All the leaders were standing in a middle of an empty room. They were all dressed in voluminous white robes. Due to the non-wall effect they appeared to be alone in a middle of a bleached universe.

"It was a terrible extinction. The Dinos have been dead for millennia. They have been converted into oil by now. This will become the main energy resource for the beginning of an industrialized world," Herr waited a few moments to allow the leaders to ponder the importance of her words.

"But there, on the planet, are chances of a suitable

evolution. The hope is we won't require these types of planetary extinction in the future," as she said this, Herr addressed a critical look toward Afronda and then Athena.

"What *positive evolution* do you want to present to us Herr?" Apoll asked.

Herr sent a mental command to the computer. Instantly, they appeared to be in the middle of a silent and peaceful planet. The sky was quite dark, but still an acceptable amount of solar light was able to penetrate down to the planet 's surface. They appeared to float in the air over top of a calm sea, close to the seaside.

Then slowly, gently, they appeared to fly to the land.

"This is a database record from 20 million years ago," Herr said. "The only animals that survived the second extinction were small mammals that were able to hide underground. Since they are omnivorous it made their survival possible. We already have some evolution, if you look here…,"

They were transported through to the image of a place with some vegetation. Strange looking animals wandered around.

"This is what I call Igga. It is larger than the original small mammals. However, it is not very well adapted to this environment. This species is extinct by now. As I said, what we are seeing now is actually an old data point, exactly 20 million years ago. One of the main reasons they died out was that there were toxic gases and this species cannot hide underground."

Herr was looking around at the audience, "Now, let's move to our time, or 40 million years after the second extinction."

The image was showing a bright blue sky and plants growing. This image was much different than the previous one.

"As you can see, the sky is clear now. The dust from the meteor impact is gone. Let us move to a different place."

For a moment the world was rushing past them, images appearing and disappearing so rapidly that they couldn't process them fast enough to perceive them clearly. Afronda had a dizzy sensation.

"Now we are in Affra. As you can see, there is high humidity here. As a result, we have this beautiful mega forest. And in the trees, these types of monkeys."

"They look like clever animals," Athena observed.

"Indeed. But not clever enough to walk away from the trees on foot to show us the greatest evolution we are looking for." Heff said ironically.

Herr turned to him and calmly she answered, "Not yet!"

Heff put his head down, embarrassed.

"When then?" Arr asked

"Quite soon," Herr replied enigmatically.

"Herr," Athena said impatiently, stepping close to her, "You posted on our shared link the details of all current living animals and plants. We can see everything there. Why have you asked for this meeting?"

Herr turned to Athena, surprised by her question. "As per the protocol we are allowed to change the variables around a particular place on the planet in order to observe its local evolution," Herr paused looking around. "I ask your permission to convert this humid place to a desert."

"As per the protocol you can proceed without asking us," Discordia said in her tiny voice.

191

"Yes," Zeu said in his booming tone, "but Herr wishes to ask our permission. She wants to watch closely how these monkeys' evolution changes if their tropical rain forest becomes arid."

"I understand what you mean," Apoll said. "This will be the biggest evolutionary step toward creating human beings and it needs to be carefully handled. Let's vote then. I am for *yes*."

———◆———

"Our weather control technology is impressive!" John said, turning his dark-skinned face to Discordia, "isn't it Ma'am?"

"Yes," Discordia approved in her tiny voice. She was looking around the control room. Due to the non-wall effect the control room appeared to be placed on the planet's surface.

"The luxurious rain forest is now a dry savannah," Emm, the big beefy guy said. He was trying to settle his large body more comfortably in the chair.

"Yes," Discordia repeated. She paused for several moments as she looked around the savannah. After a while, she observed the two control room operators were waiting for her to continue and said, "If we didn't act, these monkeys were going to be sitting complacently in their trees forever. Now they must adapt to an unfamiliar environment. Evolution means you must break some rules by forcing a change in order to adapt and survive in a hostile environment. What we are seeing right now is not only a few thousand monkeys trying to walk on two feet. It is a huge step toward human evolution," Discordia accentuated virtually every word as if she was very proud about its individual importance.

"It is remarkable indeed!" John approved. "Imagine when we come here first, it was a hostile inorganic planet."

"Indeed, the planet changed a lot," Emm was gazing around the hologram, "Ma'am, what can we do to accelerate the evolution of these monkeys to humans? I mean without violating the protocol. Otherwise, I know, we could genetically engineer them."

"You are right Emm, we are not allowed to genetically engineer them." Discordia paused for a moment to point a finger at Emm, silently saying *never think about violating the protocol.*

Emm was looking at John. They were blinking their eyes like they misunderstood.

"What is the solution to accelerate their evolution to humans then?"

In an offended tone, Discordia raised the pitch of her tiny voice and declared, "By making their environment even more hostile!"

All the leaders were seated in the amphitheater in cozy chairs. In the middle was Zeu, with Herr on his right and Poss on his left. Dem and Hest were there as well. Athena was standing down in the amphitheater in front of everyone. She was dressed in a tight white body fitting dress that looked gorgeous on her beautiful form. The dress had generous cutouts in the arms and chest area. She was waiting for Zeu's permission to speak.

"All right," Zeu said in his usual loud voice, looking

around at all the leaders. "We have two matters to discuss today. The first one is about the evolution of the new predator on the planet and will be presented by Athena," he gazed around the amphitheater, "You may begin, Athena."

Athena smiled politely and began, "As all of you well know by now, we have humans on the planet." She beamed around the room at all the leaders. "And all this occurred in a relatively quick time frame, less than sixty million years which is but a few moments compared to the time we spent stabilizing the planet, or even to the dinosaur's dynasty. I would say this is because the intermediate human-like creatures were not viable and their evolution to the final stage was accelerated by a few things," she paused again to smile at the audience.

"Specifically, I noted five types of humans. I will use, as Herr did, two words for a distinctive category. Omo Robustus, Omo Habilis, Omo Erectus, Omo Neanderthales and Omo Sapiens. Here they are."

She made a delicate hand gesture and five human holograms appeared in the middle of the amphitheater. "There are a few other intermediary Omo stages, but these five are the most notable. You can find the details of the intermediary stages at this shared link." Some blue letters appeared above the holograms showing the link's location for a few seconds, then disappeared.

Silently Athena turned to Discordia and smiled kindly at her.

"Discordia and her team did a tremendous job experimenting with the climate of the planet. As a result of converting the humid tropical forest in the middle of Affra to a dry desert, the apes were forced to leave the threes. Therefore, Omo Robustus appeared."

Athena was walking in a circle around the first ape hologram.

"It is a little developed ape that is hardly able to walk on the soil. As Discordia was generating the climate change from tropical to desert, this species was extremely unstable and died out. This gave rise to the evolution of Omo Habilis."

She moved to the next hologram. "This one has an improved vertical position, a better ability to catch objects and make primitive weapons."

She paused as she moved to the third hologram, "We obtained here on this planet our own DNA from inorganic matter. It was a long journey that took us more than 500 million years. Omo Erectus has a larger brain compared with the previous two. My detailed analysis shows that we started with an average brain size of 393 cc for Omo Robustus compared with 494 cc for Omo Habilis. A notable increase of brain capacity followed for Omo Erectus at 935 cc."

Athena gazed around the room and continued, "This is primarily because Omo Erectus changed his diet from mainly vegetables and fruits to meat. Of course, this is due to the fact they have now learned to use fire," Athena stopped abruptly as she turned first to Prom then Zeu.

"Supreme Leader Zeu, do you wish to speak now?"

"No!" Zeu answered loudly, "Please continue."

She nodded and turned back to the 3rd hologram. As she swiveled, she paused again to gaze at Prom for a few seconds. Slowly walking to the 3rd hologram she said, "The fire was protecting them from other predators and also warming their caves. It was a natural progression to cooking meat. Not the least of which, they found the meat prepared in the fire delicious."

She addressed smiles toward Dem and Hest.

"As they now have bodies adapted to travel, they are ready to seize the planet. This is possible because all the continents are still close enough to be reached. As you can see here," behind her a map of the planet appeared, "even Ausstra is able to be reached. As Discordia was experimenting with the climate of the planet a new ice age was created. Because of that this happened," Athena was walking now around the 4th hologram.

"Omo Neanderthal. He is well adapted to cold weather. He can also manufacture remarkable weapons to hunt and kill animals."

Suddenly, a rack full of primitive weapons materialized near the 4th hologram. Athena took a long javelin made of wood with a sharp stone attached to the end with twine. Athena demonstrated expert fighting moves with the javelin, dancing gracefully through the amphitheater in a bold display of power.

Afronda was wondering how such a basic weapon could become so deadly in Athena's expert hands.

Finishing her demonstration, Athena replaced the javelin on the rack, which disappeared as suddenly as it had appeared.

After a short pause, as if recovering her breath after the intense effort she made using the javelin, Athena continued, "The animals were hunted for their meat but also for their fur. With clothing made from fur the Neanderthals can survive the harsh climate. Do not forget that at the north pole the continents are united by ice and it is still possible to migrate to the Ammer continent."

She looked around the room to ensure she still had everyone's attention, saw they were watching raptly and stepped to the next hologram. "The last one is Omo sapiens."

The entire audience was looking down the amphitheater at Athena.

There is such a wonderful story to tell now, Discordia thought to herself proudly. Instead of speaking, Athena touched the hologram representing Omo sapiens. A holographic representation of its DNA appeared in front of it. With another graceful hand gesture, she created the holographic representation of her own DNA beside it.

The Omo sapiens hologram faded away, leaving only the two DNA strands. Athena pushed a DNA hologram with her left hand and the other one with her right hand until they stood beside each other. She was extremely focused on the display and by now all the people in the room were able to see the two DNA molecules were very similar.

Athena raised her eyes to the audience. Clearly, accentuating each word, she announced, "They are us."

There was a long silent moment in the amphitheater.

"Congratulations Zeu and All," Dem declared triumphantly, "We obtained our own DNA from inorganic matter and the experiment was accomplished at a planetary scale!"

"This is a monumental achievement for the experiment," Hest added. "Never before was an experiment like this conducted. We are the first."

All the people began to applaud.

"Yes," Athena agreed from her place at the front of the amphitheater.

"I remember once Herr brought to us the most stable creature of that time, a Dino.

Here, I have for you the top of the evolutionary scale of this planet."

A trapdoor opened in the floor in the middle of the amphitheater. A small platform rose up on hydraulics with a tiny form crouched upon it. Then a young girl stood, dressed modestly in fresh clothes. Her face and body were clean, and her hair was neat and tidy. At first, the child appeared scared as she looked at the people surrounding her in the amphitheater. When she finally saw Athena, her face relaxed and she appeared happy. She ran to Athena and hugged her. Athena ignored the audience as she spoke to the little girl in a strange language for a few seconds. Tenderly, Athena touched the girl's face. An apple appeared in Athena's hand through teleportation, which she then offered to the young girl. The child seemed much more comfortable and at ease now.

Turning to the audience, Athena said, "Her name is Eve. She is the most wonderful creature created on this planet. She may appear fragile, but she and her kind are now dominating the planet."

"This is remarkable!" Zeu exclaimed. It was obvious he was controlling his voice, trying not to be too loud and scare Eve.

"Does anyone have anything to say?"

"Yes!" Afronda stood up. She began to walk down the amphitheater to the little girl. With subtle gestures Afronda was rearranging her dress. She approached the young child, who appeared awestruck by Afronda's beauty.

"Athena please translate for me," Afronda requested.

She bent over the little girl. "Do you like my dress?"

The small female understood Athena's translation and she nodded to Afronda to indicate yes, she did.

"Would you like to have a dress like mine?"

Eve nodded yes, again.

"Would you like me to teach you how to make yourself beautiful?"

The young girl answered, and Athena translated for the audience, "Yes. I want that!"

Afronda turned toward the audience, declaring loudly, "We created them! We must teach them! We must interact with them!"

She was looking toward Dem and Hest as she said, "I propose an amendment to the non-interaction protocol as currently it forbids us to interact with the planet's life forms."

She anxiously looked at Zeu, then back to Dem and Hest. Finally, without saying anything further she returned to her seat.

"Athena, can you please walk little Eve out?" Zeu asked.

"Of course," Athena bent down to Eve, teaching her to make a bye-bye wave with her hand to the upper audience and they left the room.

"Before discussing any amendments, we need to debate the second agenda item of today's meeting," he said loudly. "Fire!" Zeu continued in a booming voice.

Prom had a very unhappy expression on his face. He stood and walked down to the front of the amphitheater.

By now Athena had returned and was taking a seat in the audience.

"What's going on?" Apoll asked.

"This guy," Zeu pointed to Prom, "was down on the planet's surface teaching the humans how to use fire!"

"Zeu, there is no need to overreact. The modification of non-intervention protocol is already proposed. It seems likely to be approved. I will vote yes. I want to teach planet's humans how to fight," Arr said, trying to make peace between Zeu and Prom.

"To fight?" Athena was looking ironically at Arr. "I want to teach them how to be wise!"

"I want to teach them to love the sea and how to navigate on it," Poss said.

"I want to teach them how to build great temples to venerate the sun," Apoll said.

"I want to teach them agriculture," all eyes in the room turned to Dem.

"I want to teach them what respect means," Hest said. "Yes, we will cancel the non-interaction point of the protocol immediately. We waited millennia to interact with these human beings. It is going to be so exciting. Let's vote! Dem and I are for yes too."

"Who is for?" Zeu asked.

Every single leader raised his or her hand.

"Very well then. We have permission to interact with the inhabitants of the planet. I am going to work with Dem and Hest to establish the boundaries of these interactions. Now…," Zeu was looking at Prom.

"Let's decide the fate of this guy!"

"But… he violated a law we just canceled!" Heff tried to protest.

"Silence!" Zeu screamed. "When he was down on the planet the law was still in effect. Therefore, he is guilty! This is a disciplinary case!"

"Zeu, with all due respect, there is no need to demote him from his leadership position. Despite that I understand he deserves to be punished," Discordia said in her tiny, bell-like voice.

"Okay," Prom said in a lower voice. "I am fine with your suggestion, Discordia. Prom, you should have asked first, before teaching them how to use fire."

"I assure you that you are going to remember this punishment."

"What punishment do you want to apply to him?" Herr asked.

"Physical torture!" Zeu said, looking spitefully at Prom.

"I am very adept at performing physical torture," Herr said. "Let me do this for you."

"No!" Zeu screamed. "I am going to torture him myself!" He turned to Prom as he grinned evilly.

CHAPTER 17

The message

Time afraid pyramids.

Thirteenth Student

Dem and Hest were quite uncomfortable. They were trying to enjoy aromatic tea seated around the little table near the big circular window. They were looking down to the planet.

So blue. So lovely. Dem thought to herself.

They both wished to extend this peaceful moment for a little while at least. If only to avoid the next uncomfortable discussion.

The magnetic field around the room had been increased. The room was virtually impenetrable to any kind of spy activity. *Including telepathic spying*, Hest thought, taking a long sip from her delicate tea cup, then moved her eyes from the beautiful blue planet to address Dem.

"Do you believe that bastard?"

Dem smiled at her sadly.

"Regardless … we have no choice."

"If they're concerned about us, they could find an official way to contact us! Or just come after us. They've absolutely had enough time since we left," Hest spat bitterly.

"Well, the star devices were destroyed in the very beginning, so there's no longer any official way of contacting us. The sad fact is that telepathy is the only method that might succeed," Dem looked back at Hest.

"With our advanced radio communication technology--" Hest stopped abruptly, overcome by anxiety. "I just can't believe we have to depend on him so much … again!"

"I don't like it either." Dem said keeping her voice low as she was worried it might be intercepted. "But we have no choice. Telepathic communication is the only communication method discovered so far that doesn't diminish over long distances."

"But he can lie," Hest argued.

"The possibility exists, but it is very small. He knows by now he is easily dispensable. A small mistake or even the suspicion of one, and we kill him!"

"He might not care. We treated him quite badly in the past."

"True," Dem admitted taking a sip from her tea cup. "If we suspect him, we can kill him without hesitation. But what if he's right? What he is saying does kind of make sense. Therefore, there is the possibility that he achieved a telepathic contact with his twin brain located back on our main planet. It is possible that our owner was advised of it, and he ordered us to return home."

Hest smiled bitterly at Dem.

"Indeed. It makes sense. Furthermore, we can't kill him without a full investigation."

"Yes. We know that telepathic communications of such length require a long period of intense concentration, so the instruments connected to Brain Seven could have recorded it. What we have to do now is to carefully check the records."

"Absolutely."

They sat in silence for a moment.

"Let's bring him in. He might be helpful," Hest said convinced.

Dem nodded to her and sent a mental command to the computer. The main door of the large room opened and Prom limped into the room. On his face was a profound expression of pain. He wore a large white robe that covered his body entirely. In several places the white robe was splashed with blood. Dem mentally asked the computer to show an x-ray of Prom 's body. She could see his bones were intact, but his wounds were deep, and several of them were still bleeding freely.

With a visible effort, Prom bowed before the two women.

"My ladies--"

"Oh … man," Dem started, visibly affected by Prom's dreadful appearance, "why have you not attended to your wounds? You're our main doctor. Healing your own wounds should be a priority!"

Painfully Prom smiled at them both.

"I am not permitted. Zeu doesn't allow me to take care of my injuries; he doesn't even allow me to take pain killers."

"Oh …" Dem trailed off, deeply affected.

Hest, on the other hand, gazed at him with disregard.

"This is what you deserve when you disobey the law. Zeu was right. At the time, that law as active and enforceable."

Prom's eyes moved over to Hest.

"What can I do for you ladies?"

He was still standing upright. Dem sent a mental command and a comfortable chair appeared behind him. With a delicate gesture, Dem invited him to sit. A small table also appeared beside him. A glass was on the table.

"It is a pain killer," Dem told him. "Take it. I want you to be relaxed and to pay full attention to what we are about to tell you."

Prom drank the entire contents of the glass at once. He closed his eyes and the painkiller took effect instantly. *It's so good to feel my body without pain*, he thought. It had been a considerable time now since Zeu's brutal punishment.

Finally, Prom opened his eyes. The two ladies were analyzing him.

"Thank you," he said, his eyes darting from Dem to Hest and back again. "What can I do for you now?"

"We have some … issues. We would like you to study the records of Brain Seven's activity."

"I will do my best ladies," he paused for a moment. "I though you had all the resources you needed to monitor its activity yourselves."

"We do. And have already looked at the records," Hest said firmly. "But we want you to repeat it with whatever tools you deem necessary."

"We want to see if you arrive at the same conclusion as we did, using your own methods," Dem added.

"I'll need to perform an intensive study. My primary focus has been on studying the body as a whole, not dissected brains."

"We are confident that you can handle this," Dem said.

After a short pause she continued, "We are going to ask Zeu to end his punishment."

"He will refuse!" Prom protested.

"On the contrary. He has already accepted," Hest said.

"What's going on?" Prom was baffled.

"We offered him some … concessions," Hest answered. "Not because we were forced to, but because we want to act decently. We require good results from your side, though. You will have to prove to us that our confidence in your capability is not misplaced!" Hest's voice was sharp.

Prom straightened and said, "I'm your man. You won't be disappointed." He smiled at the two women warmly. "How would you … describe the matter I have to investigate?" he added.

"Brain Seven feigns that he has established a telepathic connection with our planet of origin." Dem said on a low voice.

"This might be possible, as telepathy isn't limited by distance," Prom said convinced.

"True," Hest admitted simply. "But monitoring the electrical activity of the brain, the amount of energy consumed, the oxygen level, and other data, we might be able to determine what exactly he did."

"We might," Prom agreed.

Hest stood up. "He purports that our owner has asked us to return."

Dem raised herself up too. Looking down at Prom she said, "We need to determine if this is truly what our owner demands."

The little ship entered the planet's atmosphere. Poss loved driving it so much. Looking back to Zeu and Herr he said, "As we have some extra time, I would like to show you the deepest place on this planet."

"You enjoy going underwater so much," Herr observed.

"Yes! Always!" Poss said gleefully.

"And why exactly you want to show us this place?" He inquired.

Zeu interjected, "Some gossip suggests that we might need to abandon this planet soon. If so, we need to hide some monitoring equipment, or a terminal Star Gate device, possibly deep undersea, as Poss suggested."

"True!" Herr admitted, "Also, in a few thousand years, they will have become sufficiently technologically advanced to observe a huge object like our space ship in their sky. Therefore, we need to move far away, where we can't be observed. At such a safe distance, classical teleporting systems won't be functional, and a Star Gate will be the only way to communicate and transport with the planet instantly." Herr said, as she looked down to the sea.

The little ship was now dipping beneath the sea's surface.

"It's going to take time to them to develop the technology necessary to penetrate as deep as this hole. I call it Marinny's hole. Because of its depth, we can hide our equipment here quite well. It will remain concealed for a while at least, and it will auto-destruct without any trace when and if it's necessary," Prom said, convinced.

"True," Herr admitted. "If I recall correctly, this was the place Heff chose to send his equipment when we asked him to move the tectonic plates."

"Yes," Zeu said so that only Herr could hear. "He is

very busy now. I asked him to start building new Star Gate devices that we can install at intervals on our way home so that we can maintain an instant link back to this planet. No mistakes this time. He bet his life on this."

"We need to be able to communication instantly once we leave the planet," Herr retorted to Zeu. As usual, she approved of him utterly.

Poss was fully engrossed in admiring the aquatic landscape. Light was not able to penetrate this deep, and as a result, the ship's lighting system had automatically activated. The passengers were able to see their surroundings as though illuminated by daylight.

"Not too much life here," Herr observed.

"True, but I'm sure you already have some ideas to genetically modify a few species and make this ocean bottom more populated," Poss observed contentedly.

"Yes, sure. At least it will be something for me to do." Herr smiled politely at Poss.

"Okay bro! Good enough. Let's go to the Affra continent now. They're waiting for us." Zeu said.

"Okay!" Poss started to take the ship back to the surface.

"Discordia said she will not be able to attend this meeting as she wanted to inspect the SG devices. Also Prom might be not able to attend the meeting," Zeu noted. "He says he's busy with his new job."

"Yes," Herr smiled nicely to him. "He's keeping Brain Seven under constant observation while he conducts his investigation."

With a splash, the little ship breached the surface of the water. After a quick flight they arrived at Affra continent. From the sky, they could see the Sphinx statue.

"Oh … it's built already," Poss observed wonderingly.

"Yes," Herr said. "I forgot to tell you. However, you seemed more interested in mapping the ocean floors and such."

Poss didn't rise to the bait. He was too intently focused on landing the little ship on the plateau by the big Sphinx Statue. Examining their surroundings, Herr informed Zeu, "Herm, Apoll, Arr and Athena are here."

"Yes, it was their team who calculated everything and built this statue."

Once the ship had landed, Zeu, Herr and Poss disembarked. They sat in front of the Sphinx statue and surveyed the surrounding landscape. The group of five approached them.

"Be welcome!" Athena smiled politely at them. Herr bent his head and smiled politely in acknowledgement.

Zeu was looking around, "we cannot start the meeting yet. As you know, this is not a mandatory meeting, therefore not all the leaders will attend it. But Dem and Hest have said they will participate, so we have to wait for them. Are you confident that we are safe here?" Zeu addressed the question to Arr.

"Yes," Arr answered promptly. "I scanned the area. All clear. What you see around you are our humanoid robots. The current humans can't distinguish our robots from humans. The robots are here for our protection, no real humans will be allowed to enter this perimeter now. The robots will keep them away until our meeting is concluded."

"Perfect!" Zeu approved.

A small noise made them all look in the same direction. Three bodies began to materialize trough teleportation.

Dem, Hest, and Afronda had clearly chosen to teleport to the meeting. There was another noise, and several more people materialized – a small group of students. Student Number 13 was with them. He stood out starkly compared to the other students, who appeared young and handsome. In contrast, his white hair and long white beard made Number 13 look old despite the fact that he kept his body in wonderful condition.

"Welcome Ladies," Zeu said as he approached the small group.

The women were dressed in long white robes, which fluttered appealingly in the light breeze.

"What wonderful weather!" Afronda observed happily.

"Yes, and quite humid," Hest approved.

"Just before you arrived here, there was a little rain," Athena informed them.

"A little rain," Dem said with a smile, while also managing to convey disapproval. "Discordia said this will be a desert soon."

"Then … I can see a mistake," a voice piped up from the group of students.

Everyone turned to Student Number 13.

"What mistake are you talking about?" Athena asked him loudly.

Not intimidated by Athena's volume, he continued, "According to your plans, the main pyramids will be built here. I have seen Discordia's forecast. The climate is rapidly becoming arid here, and it's very possible that by the time we start building the pyramids, this will already be a desert."

"So what?" Athena was clearly irritated by his observations.

"After many years, the advanced society of this planet will observe two different kinds of erosion: the Sphinx will have been eroded by precipitation, but the pyramids will not. Therefore, they will be able to correctly deduce that they were built at different times."

"Yes. But this is what we want," Athena retorted, still irritated.

"Oh... I though you wanted the Sphinx and the pyramid complex to appear as though they were built simultaneously ..." Student Number 13 said, stroking his long white beard.

"Not at all." Athena said, shooting him a reproachful glare.

"Well," Herm began, trying to make peace between the two of them, "they need to understand that the Sphinx is the master piece of this puzzle. It was taking me some time to figure out all these intriguing details."

"Let's start at the beginning!" Zeu demanded.

"Yes." Herm said, bending his head toward Zeu. "As was approved in an earlier meeting, we want to leave them some keys ... some signs. These will deepen and sharpen their knowledge. The signs will be a message; directions, if you will, that will lead them to us."

"We approved of this as these beings are not just a simple experiment for us," Dem said. "They are – their civilization is like a young member of our family. When they are mature enough, we want them to have some clues regarding how we influenced this planet, and therefore their own evolution. Also, as was already mentioned, this message will show them how to find us. When they decode the message, it will doubtless be a challenge for their primitive technology to travel within the universe, but it will also be a motivation. Once they will find us, a new stage of this experiment and a new milestone in their evolution will also be achieved. You may continue Herm," Dem smiled benignly at Herm.

"certainly, ma'am," Herm said respectfully. "They will observe that there are edifices scattered around their planet that could not have been built by the society of the time. Take these monuments, for example. They could not be built by them as their society is not developed at all. In fact, they are in the stone age right now," Herm looked around at his audience. "Connecting each of these edifices, we are going to build a sky map; a map that they should be able to understand once their civilization is sufficiently advanced. The monuments will be built in a precise circle around the planet. The distance between these places will suggest their mathematical proportions and relationships. If they are able to understand the proportions, this map will lead them to us. As you can see, the Sphinx is the master piece of this puzzle. As such, I call it the Guardian. We know that their galaxy cycles once every 26,000 years. On the precise date of the next rotation, the eyes of the Sphinx ... " he paused, gazing at the group of students and mainly Student Number 13, "are directed to our galaxy and our primary planet."

"Quite easy," Apoll observed.

Afronda stepped towards him, "Why did you choose such a figure as the key puzzle piece? I find it quite ..." she trailed off, appearing to search for a suitable word.

"Unpleasant?" Apoll suggested, trying to help her.

"Yes, unpleasant." Afronda concurred. "We need visual harmony here. I am not sure I perceive that harmony, looking at this statue."

"There are two key messages here," Arr stepped in as though his friend Apoll was in danger. "Within the current animal kingdom on this planet, the lion is the strongest animal. You could call him the king of the animals."

"Then why didn't you just build a lion statue?" Afronda asked, refusing to accept that this statue must remain the key piece of the puzzle as it was built now.

"Because we also need to leave no doubt in their minds that this also has something to do with mankind," Athena waded into the discussion. "And so here we are. The Sphinx is a lion with a human head, gazing at our planet of origin."

"We still need visual harmony," Afronda insisted. Evidently she was not entirely satisfied by their explanation.

After a moment of silence Herm continued. "There are going to be pyramids around the planet, reflecting the proportion of our populated worlds. Once they decode it, they're going to have a quite well-constructed astronomical map." Herm proudly provided details. "In addition, we have plans to build what is called Nazza plateau in Ammer, in Perr. I have the drawings here. However, these various designs will be visible from the sky only, and not from the ground." He paused and looked to Apoll, "you might want to give some details regarding the construction of these massive edifices Apoll."

Apoll stepped in, nodding. "We will use local rock, as in Affra. All the rocks will be arranged in perfect triangles for the pyramid's construction. The rocks will be so precisely aligned that there will be practically no distance between blocks. In the end, almost 5 billion blocks will be used to build each pyramid, and each will be perfectly aligned to magnetic north. We will also build other pyramids in

Amerr; our current drawings place them at Macuu Picuu. We will also build pyramids in Assa, and so on. We even have plans to build undersea pyramids. All of them will be earthquake proof, so that they remain on the planet's surface over the eons," Apoll said proudly, looking around.

"We want them to be a witness to our powers. We will place the pyramids quite close to the current planet's equator. However, there may be a deviation of up to 30 degrees due to natural tectonic movement. We expect that it will only be a matter of several thousand years before their society has reached a sufficient level of advancement to analyze the pyramids scattered around the planet." He paused for moment to give the others some time to this information.

"The entire complex can be seen from space and from the planet's moon," Herm added.

"Unlike our plans for the pyramids, the Sphinx was not assembled piece by piece. Instead, it was carved from a single massive slab of limestone. We left very few clues about its construction, and over time it will be submerged beneath the desert's sand to remain buried for most of its life. This will preserve it and save it from destruction. We took this extra precaution as we need it to be intact when their civilization has attained the degree of advancement required to decode it. However, we plan to proceed differently with the construction of pyramids. Our robots will handle the heavy blocks required. They are already assembling over there." And Apoll pointed to several groups of people that were in fact robots. "As you can see, they look identical to the current habitants of the planet. We intend to collaborate with current local kings and let it appear as though the local kings had somehow contributed to the construction of the pyramids. However, we will influence their leaders to respect the constructor workers. As a result, their meals will be fabulous."

"Okay, okay we don't need that much detail for now," Zeu interrupted him. "If we wish, I presume we can find all these details in the common shared drive?" He shot an interrogative look at Apoll, who nodded back in reply.

"Maybe you want to address mathematics and other messages now?" Zeu said as he felt Apoll was anxious to talk about this too.

"Sure thing Zeu," Apoll beamed his beautiful face around at the others.

"We will build three great pyramids on the Gizz plateau. The masterpiece of all the pyramids will be the Great Pyramid. At the equinox, its eight faces will be visible to the naked eye for a few brief seconds."

"At least they can precisely determine when the equinox is," Afronda interrupted in an ironic voice.

As if impervious to her irony, Apoll continued. "The greatest pyramid of Gizz will be here, in the center of it all, indicating where our planet of origin is. The master pyramid will provide them with very powerful knowledge about their own planet. It will be 73.5 units long and 20 units in height. Facing the sun rise, the first hypotheses might be that it is dedicated to the Sun God," He paused proudly and looked around.

Afronda couldn't stop herself from thinking, *how selfish! Dedicated to the Sun God or to himself? He knows he will be venerated as the God of the Sun across all earth cultures.*

After relishing in his moment of victory, Apoll was shook

his long blond tresses and continued: "The mathematical relationships around the pyramid are based on pi and the golden number or golden ratio. The golden number occurs all over the world: in animals, proportions of the human body, astrology, and all over the pyramids. It is a constant of the universe. These equations and relationships are embedded within the pyramids themselves. There are mathematical messages hidden in them, like the speed of rotation of their planet, the speed of light, and so on. The interior temperature of Great Pyramid will be kept constant at the average temperature of earth, or 20 universal temperature degrees. We also took the step of including warnings as about some potential natural disasters. For example they will be able to calculate the rotation of the planet's core and therefore when it will stop, or when their planet will be consumed by solar radiation. These pose serious potential threats."

"In other words what you're saying," Athena tried to arrive at a conclusion, "is that the humans won't be able to ignore so many coincidences. There will be too much precision to believe that the ancients built the monuments on this plateau, let alone understood the mathematics behind them."

"Exactly," Apoll replied in an animated tone. "The message will be transmitted through mathematics. We are going to use a specially proposed series of numbers. Each of these together, including the mysterious alignment of the pyramids, is designed to provoke the human mind." He looked around proudly.

"The pyramids will gleam in the light of the sun. Crossing the parallels and meridians of their planet, humans will perceive that the Great Pyramid is located exactly in the middle of the earth and aligned precisely northward."

"Also," Herm added, "it will be easy for them to find the mathematic relationship between the perimeter of the bottom of this pyramid and the sun's radius. There will be sophisticated underground tunnels and pathways comparable to a microcosmic model of the relationship. It will be an impressive underground network."

"But," Hest added, "I suggested paying special attention to Easter Island as it is the most isolated place on the planet. I recommended placing 60 heavy statues weighing as much as 200 tons each. Their very presence will incite the curiosity of the humans."

"They will be added," Zeu confirmed to Hest.

"Some further details regarding construction," Herm said in a low voice, looking toward Zeu as though imploring him for permission to speak. Zeu said nothing, so Herm continued, "we plan to build the Great Pyramid in 20 years. The access door of the pyramid will weigh 20 tons but it will be so well balanced that it will open with minimal force. All lighting will be provided by electric power generation, not flame. The mortar we are using will be stronger than the stones themselves. The humans might be able to learn its chemical formula. Complex tools need to be used to accomplish all of this," He concluded convincingly.

"Is there anything more?" Zeu looked around inquiringly.

"Generally," Herr began, "there will be no inscriptions inside any of the pyramids. In the underground tunnels and surroundings there will be inscriptions, and they will have a very high level of difficulty. The humans might never agree on their meaning. Also the pyramids should not be confused as being the tombs of the kings."

"All of these details will be a mysterious message from the past, and they will understand our contribution to their civilization. Also, in the worst-case scenario that we lose contact and our database of this side of the universe, it will be easy to determine we were here via elementary planetary scanning and detection of these pyramid alignments. Actually, it happened once on our way here, when we lost all the Star Gate devices due to the act of sabotage. We hope this will never be repeated." She directed her gaze at Zeu as if to say, *you are responsible.* "But we prefer to take all possible precautions," Dem concluded, smiling.

"Well, everything sounds good to us. But now, we are going to have a little private meeting. Would you please excuse us?" Dem continued to smile politely at the leaders.

"Zeu and Herr, if you don't mind, can you walk with us?" Hest said. Her face was quite bitter.

"Oh, ladies! Please," Herr said, protesting. "There is nothing to hide!"

"What's going on?" Arr asked. He was ready to react, as though preparing for an attack.

"Herr is pregnant!" Hest said in a loud, accusing voice. "The child is Zeu's."

"What?" Herm was bewildered. Almost all the leaders were perplexed as well. For a moment, there was silence.

"But ... this is illegal!" Afronda said in consternation.

"No," Herr said, trying to convince her. "It isn't illegal. It *is* highly irregular and frowned upon. But it is not strictly illegal."

"It is not illegal--" Zeu interjected. " Dem, Hest: you

are here to make sure the law, regulations and protocols are respected. This is not an illegal act. Therefore, can you conclude this meeting?"

Dem and Hest smiled at him bitterly. "The meeting is adjourned." Dem said.

CHAPTER 18

Ancient Gods

Sometimes all that remains are just a few lovely legends.

Diane

"Look at her," Dem said.

Hest bent down to the holographic record. "She is so full of energy because she is so young," Hest said.

"So young you say? She's more than a thousand years old. In other words, without life extension treatments she would've died a hundred times by now."

"What I mean is, she's young compared to us. We traveled through millennia due to our immortality. Compared to us, Diane – Zeu and Herr's daughter – is quite young."

"I would say her energy is also related to her genetics. Bot her parents are full of energy."

"Perhaps one can make the argument that natural breeding is not all that bad."

"Maybe," Dem said, unconvinced. "Diane is a lovely

example of success, but we know from our own history how many failures, issues, and problems were connected with children that were not carefully projected by our computers. Now our computers take all possible genetic combinations and their potential effects into consideration. All is carefully calculated. Nothing is left to chance."

Hest smiled at Dem.

"I agree. Diane was a risk. I am happy that she appears acceptable. So far, at least."

The two ladies turned back to the hologram showing Diane down on the planet in a wood, hunting with a bow and arrows. The hologram showed that it was night there, with a full moon lending a silvery shimmer of light to the forest.

"She loves to hunt."

"She loves the moon."

"She is the supreme symbol of hunting and the moon, for those mortal humans who currently inhabit the planet."

"Yes. But, we still have to complete our report to our owner explaining this … incident."

"Diane's birth. If we write the report well, I expect our owners will accept Zeu and Herr's apologies."

<hr>

"The stories about us are grossly distorted and not well understood," Diane said to Apoll. They were seated by the glass window with a direct view to the blue planet below. The planet appeared to be a delicate blue balloon floating in a dark universe. Diane was dressed in a white gown that was well fitted on her shapely body. It was a very short dress; so short in fact that had she been down on the planet below, the people there might have been shocked at her improper attire. The standards for women's dress in Greece – the most civilized place on earth at the time – were much more modest, and consisted of a long, loose white dress.

Apoll was dressed in a golden yellow suit worn very tight on his body. The metallic suit appeared to be actually made of gold. It created harmony nicely on his wonderfully-proportioned body with his long curly blond hair and blue eyes.

"Yes. I agree," Apoll said, "the stories about us are distorted. They think that we are brother and sister. So wrong ... I was conceived through the artificial combination of two molecules carefully calculated to arrive at this exact form, and you were naturally conceived by an ancient method that I thought has ceased to exist on this stage of our civilization."

"Actually, I don't blame them," Diane smiled sweetly at Apoll, "our faces do resemble each other closely."

"A simple coincidence," Apoll dismissed her abruptly. "I think the main fact is that they perceived your deep love of the night and the moon. I am your opposite, I hate the night. I love the day, the sun. We represent a drama of characters in opposition."

They stopped their chat for a moment to look down together at the planet.

"I am sorry Diane," Apoll said politely, "but I find it inappropriate for a young girl to spend her nights alone in the woods."

"I like to hunt!" Diane answered him with an ironic smile. "And the best time to hunt is at night."

"And I think you are ignorant to danger," Apoll answered sharply.

"Not at all." Diane argued. "I always wear anti-gravity shoes, I'm always in contact with the teleportation system, I always carry motion sensors …"

"I see," Apoll interrupted her. "You're saying that you can feel the wild animals with the sensors, you can fly with anti-gravity shoes, you can appear or disappear trough the teleportation system, and so on. Quite remarkable for a girly creature like you." Apoll smiled as though he'd made a good joke. "And yet, you still use a bow and arrows when you hunt," he paused for a long moment to emphasize his criticism. "Quite primitive."

"I like to hunt using a bow and arrow. I feel so much closer to these people – people who in fact have the same DNA as us. I feel that had I been born there on the planet in these times, I would have been able to survive by myself." She nodded convincingly at Apoll.

"Ignorant to danger," she repeated Apoll's words slowly, suddenly coming to a realization. "You've been checking in on me like an older brother. I always have a laser gun with me too. However, so far I've never had to it. The bow and arrows have been enough."

"Okay," Apoll smiled indulgently. "Don't use the laser at all; Zeu has driven the planet's inhabitants crazy by over-using his huge laser gun."

"Yes," Diane agreed sadly. "Actually, he modified his to make a terrible booming noise when it is used."

"He's also very ostentatious in his use of teleportation, as well as flying right in front of people with anti-gravitaty shoes."

"Herm also overdoes the anti-gravitaty shoes," Apoll said somewhat accusingly.

"I think we are all making mistakes. All of us. We should not be intervening so brutally with their civilization."

"We don't," Apoll said. "Diane, you were born quite recently. You don't know what it's like to wait next to a lifeless planet for long, boring millennia, waiting for some intelligent creatures to be formed there. Now that they're here, we feel a natural impulse to interact with them. That's why the non-interaction protocol was amended. It is now legal to interact with them."

Diane gazed at him dubiously.

"You said that they saw me hunting at night. On the contrary, they notice you, a handsome blond always flying about, singing, teaching them arts and architecture. That appears to me like a gross intervention."

"But don't they deserve our teachings?" Apoll asked in protest.

"But …"

"But what?" Apoll was angry now.

"Just that you talk with them too much. You share too many of our predictions."

Apoll began to protest but instead remained silent. Shortly thereafter, he resumed.

"Then I'll leave Greece and teach the people to build an invincible city and how to live there in peace."

After another short pause, he continued, "Dem and Hest are interacting with the planet's habitants too. Dem is teaching them agriculture, and Hest is quite involved in politics. You don't have to feel guilty for your own interactions Diane."

"I know," Diane concurred. "I said that *all of us* are interacting too much."

"Yes. And that new guy..." Apoll made an effort to remember his name, "the former student – he used to be called Number 7."

"Now he is Dionn," Diane said smiling

"Dionn." Apoll said disgusted. "Always drunk, and always with them."

"It is easy to teach the people of earth to drink!" Diane said and she started to laugh.

"I don't understand why Dem and Hest added him to the leadership team. He is so... irresponsible." Apoll was quite frustrated now. He tried to calm himself down by watching the delicate blue planet. Finally he turned to Diane. "And ... your parents, they have serious problems."

"They do," Diane admitted simply.

———————

Zeu and Herr were seated by the huge ship's window looking down to the blue planet. Herr was trying to think about lovely things like, *from the planet, our ship looks like a shiny star,* but in reality, she was really angry.

"For now, your new issue is Hecul," Zeu said moving his eyes from the blue planet to Herr.

"Why are you so protective of him?" Herr questioned him in a sharp voice.

"Because, he carries my DNA." Zeu answered impolitely.

"I would hazard a guess that there are a good many bastards carrying your DNA down there on the planet. All of them thanks to your irresponsible actions. What makes this one so special then?" Herr was becoming angrier.

"Why do you hate Hecul in particular so much?"

Herr didn't answer. For a moment they waited in silence.

"I'd wager you hate him because he is such an achievement of genetics. He is powerful. Strong. Handsome. Very well built. Almost perfect." Zeu tried to guess at the reasons for Herr's hatred.

"If so, I have to test him." Herr answered, with a sinister smile at Zeu.

CHAPTER 19

The Incident

*So much pain. So much suffering.
And so little hope.*

Pan Dora – Secret journal

The little white amphitheater was situated in the middle of a white universe; an infinite white space. Inside the amphitheater were 31 people dressed in loose white robes. A young woman whose beauty rivaled Afronda's stood in the middle of the amphitheater. Her name was Pan Dora. She gazed at the rest of the other students with her in the amphitheater; all of them were young and handsome, with one singular exception: Student Number 13. He stood out from the others not because he was ugly – in fact he was quite handsome – but because of his long white hair and beard, for which he refused to provide a logical explanation. Also, while all the other students had by now chosen their own names, he was still only known as Student Number 13. And while he didn't object to being called by his number, he fully supported his peers when they chose names for themselves, particularly Pan Dora, who had formerly been known as Student Number 18. In fact, he had great admiration for Pan Dora.

Appearing philosophical, Pan Dora took a few steps down into the amphitheater and finally began to speak. "There are 31 of us now. None of the rest of us was as fortunate as our former colleague, Student Number 7, who has been promoted to the rank of leader for this experiment. As you well know, he has taken the name Dionn and is known as the god of wine and partying in the country of Greecee."

"No regrets, Pan Dora. Just one less drunk fellow," Ex-student 9 said in a funny voice, leaning down towards Pan Dora. He was a good-looking guy with long dark hair and hazel eyes.

She smiled up at him, then looked around at her audience.

"I'd like to thank you all for attending this meeting and being confident in my ability to organize secret meetings such as this one," She paused, scanning the amphitheater with her pretty eyes.

"And I have specifically included you," at this, she looked directly at Student Number 13, "as you missed several meetings."

He returned her gaze frankly. "You are an excellent leader Pan Dora. You must know by now how much I admire you."

She smiled at him in silent thanks and continued, "This arrangement is as secret as it can be. As you know, we're not hiding because of Dem and Hest, but I have still not told them anything yet." She paused and looked up to the students sated in the amphitheater. "We are, however, certainly hiding because of Zeu. In normal circumstances, I might worry that Apoll would figure something out with his sophisticated computers and software algorithms. But at present, he is distracted by his new mega city project."

"How about Zeu himself?" A pretty female student inquired, "He's also very good at figuring these things out."

"I asked Herr to watch him and to make sure he surmises nothing," replied Pan Dora looking convincingly back at the student, whose name was Anna. She had previously been known as Student 19.

"What you're saying then, is that Herr is manipulating us," Anna shot back.

"Not exactly. But she wouldn't mind if we took over control of the experiment. You see, Herr hates Zeu because he's betrayed her so many times with young girls on the planet."

"But--" A young man named Saull, who had been known as Student 17, interjected, his voice full of emotion, "Pan Dora ... do you think we're ready?"

"Of course we are! If we're going to do this, you all need to put more trust in your own powers and abilities! Besides, the way Zeu and his team are handling this planet is disappointing. I am absolutely confident we can do a much better job."

"But--" Saull tried to protest again. He was cut short before finishing his sentence by the sudden appearance Zeu's hologram in the middle of the amphitheater.

A sudden murmur rippled through the students, looks of sheer terror on their faces. Zeu's hologram swiveled directly to Pan Dora and said, "Student Number 18; would you mind coming to my office?"

Pan Dora answered back in a normal voice, "That won't be a problem."

As suddenly as it had appeared, Zeu's hologram vanished.

A cold silence flooded the amphitheater for several seconds. Normally, an incident of this magnitude would have provoked considerable discussion, but now the silence was profound. No one dared say anything, as it was obvious this room was not as safe as Pan Dora had implied at the beginning of their clandestine meeting.

Down in the amphitheater, Pan Dora stood calmly. She moved her eyes around the Amphitheater. "I can handle this. I will take the blame." She started to walk away.

Everyone looked down at Pan Dora as she headed toward the amphitheater's exit. No one could articulate a word yet.

"You are very brave, Pan Dora!" Student Number 13 said admiringly.

She turned and inclined her head towards him, as if to say, *thank you.*

Pan Dora entered the bullet elevator. With a mental command, she set the elevator's destination for Zeu's main office. When the doors opened, Pan Dora was amazed at the massive size and luxury of the office.

Zeu was seated at his desk; Herr stood near him.

This is too many surprises for a single day, Pan Dora thought. It was clear to her now that Herr was on Zeu's side. *I was so stupid to trust her.*

It took a while for Pan Dora to walk the length of the

room to Zeu's desk, giving her time to deeply regret her misplaced faith in Herr.

"You wanted to see me?" Pan Dora inquired in a normal voice.

Zeu didn't respond. His face clearly expressed his disgust. Pan Dora shifted her gaze to Herr.

"I have nothing to do with this," Herr said firmly.

Pan Dora shot Herr a bitter smile. "It's okay. As a woman, I understand you." Pan Dora replied.

Herr was clearly unsatisfied, but preferred not to say more and walked away from Zeu's desk.

"I didn't give you permission to walk away!" Zeu roared in a terrifying voice.

"Very well then," Herr said calmly, and turned back.

"Zeu, I understand you are angry, but screaming won't intimidate me," Pan Dora said, struggling to maintain her customary calm voice. "I'm sure you can show some degree of respect, even in a difficult situation." She paused, but Zeu said nothing. "Also, I believe--"

But her sentence was abruptly cut off as Zeu interrupted, " And I believe that you are terribly naive, Student 18!"

"My name is Pan Dora," she interrupted, impolitely this time.

Zeu was pounded his fist on his desk in fury, "You may call yourself whatever you want, but it's only a nickname. Officially, you are Student 18. You're nothing but a number. And you're very, very naive."

He paused for a long moment, as if trying to calm himself down.

"However, what I can't understand in this situation is how all the other new students could be so naive as well."

"Then don't believe it. Believe I manipulated them and therefore I am the only guilty party." Pan Dora fought to keep her tone calm and even.

"I will accept that," Zeu said. It was evident that he was also struggling with himself to keep his voice calm.

"So … what's next then?" Pan Dora asked simply. "Are you going to punish me, or what?"

"Yes! Of course!" Zeu answered in an animated voice. His eyes gleamed with anticipation.

"I have something that I want to test on the planet's inhabitants. And you," he smiled cruelly at Pan Dora, "will be my carrier." In an instant he had jumped over his massive desk and hit Pan Dora's neck with the side of his forearm. Pan Dora had no time to react. She dropped to the floor, unconscious.

⸻⸺◆⸺⸻

Pan Dora woke up alone on the seashore.

The ocean, the waves, the weather – everything was so beautiful. After surveying her surroundings, she realized she was on a very large island. She couldn't be sure yet, however, if it was reality or just a holographic simulation. In the distance she saw another strip of land, but she couldn't be certain if it was another island or the main continent. Suddenly, a shiver ran down her spine, and Zeu's words 'you will be my carrier' boomed in her ears. *For sure this is reality*, Pan Dora knew. She tried to bend her head to look down at herself but she realized that, except for her legs, the rest of her body seemed to be paralyzed. *It's a drug*, a faint voice echoed in her mind.

Vaguely, she recalled herself immobile on a table in the

ship's laboratory. An articulated robotic arm with a syringe moved slowly toward her. The syringe contained a green liquid. *The drug that keeps me paralyzed right now*, Pan Dora thought. She felt no pain. Everything seemed fine, except that she could only move her legs and her eyes. She realized with terror that she could no longer communicate mentally with her computer. She was abandoned on this island, totally alone and without any possibility of communication with the ship. The microchip was still functioning, having stored a lot of data: her personal memories, and many other pieces of information. It was acting as a computer, but an isolated one. One that was no longer connected to the ship's network, or any other network for that matter. A sigh flooded Pan Dora's brain, but she decided to be brave and not to be intimidated by Zeu's miserable tricks. *I am stronger than he imagines!* Pan Dora tried to give herself courage. *He's in for a big surprise soon.*

Pan Dora looked down at herself as much as possible, while only being able to move her eyes. She realized she was dressed in a lovely long white robe that made her wonderful body look tempting.

Suddenly she became agitated. In her left hand she held a box. It was a medium-sized box, but one with a large lock on it. '*You will be my carrier,*' she remembered Zeu's with apprehension. Despite the fact that it looked like a simple box that could have been made on the planet, Pan Dora knew that it had originated on the ship and was hermetically sealed.

She tried with a desperate effort to send a message to her computer. Nothing. *What could be in that hermetically sealed box?* Pan Dora racked her brain to the point of pain, or maybe it was the mental effort of trying to contact her computer that was causing her head to hurt. *Either way,* she reasoned, *I have to figure this out. I appeared here holding a hermetically sealed box in my hand. What might it contain?*

Suddenly, she felt the impulse to scream, but couldn't open her mouth because of the paralytic effects of the drug. *The box contains viruses,* she realized with a shiver of fear. *Deadly viruses. This box is a biological weapon.* Pan Dora felt herself begin to sweat. *The box. Biological warfare. Zeu wants to release the virus inside the planet's atmosphere … on this very island. The entire population of the island will die if the virus is released,* she could feel the sweat trickle down her neck, *and … will I die along with them? No. I should have been immunized for this virus. He wants me to watch it happen, live through the micro-camera implanted in my right eye, like some kind of sick show. He wants me to see them all die.*

She noticed that the micro-camera implanted in her right eye was still working normally. The eye micro-camera was actually a mandatory device as the microchip. *Zeu can see everything I see.* With a desperate effort she tried to shake her body and drop the box in the sand. Her body wouldn't obey her commands, however, and the box was still there, grasped firmly in her left hand. *It's the drug.* Pandora tried to calm herself. She decided to walk around, to find a silent and isolated place. She would stay there as long as she could, in hopes that the effects of the drug would diminish in time. Then, when she could move enough, she would bury the box deep down in the earth in hopes that it would never be found, and the viruses never released.

"Are you feeling all right, beautiful girl?"

Normally her face would have shown wonder at this,

but the drug had frozen her face muscles. For the moment, her face was expressionless.

"You are so beautiful – like Aphrodite – born from the sea's foam," A young attractive young man knelt near her in the sand. The drug must have dulled her senses so that they weren't functioning normally. Otherwise, she would have noticed him immediately.

The young man addressed Pan Dora in one of the languages of earth, which she had no trouble understanding, as she was highly proficient in all languages spoken on the planet. If the drug had not locked her mouth shut, she would have been able to answer him.

He continued his chatter, and reached down to help her to walk, as he realized by now that there was something wrong with her. With evening approaching, he decided to bring the strange beautiful girl to his village to protect her, for it wasn't safe alone on the shore at night. Walking to the village, Pan Dora took note of the crops growing in little garden plots. There were tomatoes, cucumbers, beans, and … was that garlic? Yes, fresh garlic! *They should have dried garlic from last year's crop*, she realized. Tears of relief sprang to her eyes.

There is hope.

The young man wondered why the beautiful girl was crying. For herself, after a life that had spanned millennia, Pan Dora didn't realize it was possible anymore for her to be so excited by the simple miracle of hope that she would shed tears.

When they arrived at the house of the young man, Pan Dora decided to sleep in hopes that it would make the drug weaker and she could be herself again. As she fell asleep, her eyes fixed on the rope of dried garlic hanging on the opposite wall. She dreamed of garlic that night, and she slept the sleep of the earth.

———◈———

Herr walked through the intricate hologram and Zeu followed her carefully. They were so intent on the hologram, that they paid no attention when Prom entered. The hologram showed a complicated genetic structure, then the projection switched to show parts of the human body with terrible inflammation. The abscesses looked terrible. It was a disgusting image. Some of the abscesses were bleeding, and others oozed a yellow, viscous fluid that signified advanced infection.

"Why my son?" Prom demanded, angrily looking at Zeu.

"Why not your son?" Zeu answered back in a calm voice.

"If it was your son, you would be very affected," Prom tried to control the emotion his voice.

"You know what? You are pathetic! Both of you!" Herr said, her voice dripping with disapproval. Turning to Prom, she sent a mental command to her computer, and the huge hologram disappeared. Now they stood in a middle of a huge empty room.

She fixed Prom with her gaze, "Which of his sons you are referring to?"

"Herr, I am sorry. I have heard about your jealousy. But, just now we're discussing--"

"We should be discussing the law," Herr barked in a

load voice. "Law and order. It appears both of you need to read the official regulations of this mission again."

She paused, gazing at them each in turn. "The official documents state clearly that we *may* interact with the habitants of the planet, but only *within reasonable limits*. If a child is procreated, it must remain there on the planet." She was looked ironically back to Zeu and to Prom, "In other words, don't bother me with your bastards." Now she was screaming.

"I don't want to her about Hercules, Lyc, Pea or any of your other many bastards. They must to pay, along with the rest of the planet's inhabitants. Or perhaps they should pay even more. After all, they are nothing more than mistakes in my mind."

Having said her piece, she turned her back on them and walked to the room's large window. From there she looked down at the beautiful blue planet.

Zeu and Prom remained where they stood, silently looking after her.

Finally, Zeu said, "Herr is correct. Respecting official regulations is absolutely mandatory for you. And even for me."

"Yes. You should be a role model," Prom said, "that is, if you want to maintain order."

"Of course I want order," Zeu shot back.

"You will both do your best to maintain order," Herr said sternly, walking back to them. "I'll be watching you." She moved closer to Zeu and whispered in his ear:

"I'll be watching you."

It was the third day since Pan Dora's arrival on the island. She tried to rest, to sleep as much as possible, and to eat. The food they gave her was simply made. But despite being humble, it was very tasty. Grilled chicken, the boiled seafood, the vegetable salad, the bean soup and many other dishes were delicious. She wondered, giggling to herself, if the people of the island knew that the chicken's grandfather was the mighty dinosaur itself. Pan Dora also tried to eat more fresh fruit every day. By now she felt quite strong, and the effect of the drug was almost gone. She could walk, she could move her hands, she could think freely.

The house was more like a little cave on the island's rock. It consisted of a main room with two other little cavern-like rooms to either side. One was a bedroom for Pea (the young man who had rescued her from the beach) and the other one for his mother, Asia.

As comfortable as she was in Pea's home, Pan Dora intensely missed her connection with the main computer on the ship. She missed having access to the database, the instant communication, and many other technical features. Since the connection with her computer had been cut by Zeu, Pan Dora could only count on her own brain and the microchip implanted there. Suddenly, she felt the cold knife of fear at her throat. *The box. The biological weapon. Where was it?* Desperately she looked around the room. With a surge of relief, she noticed it sitting safely in a corner. The big lock was still firmly affixed to the box. She perceived that Zeu was quite diabolical in his plan. He had devised a small, rustic box with a big complex lock. Quite a tempting target, actually. Anyone would be curious to know what was inside. Pan Dora tried to think of a way she could hide the box. Better yet, to bury safely it in a hidden place. *The island should be safe. For a while, at least.* After it was hidden, she could look for another solution, *maybe I could burn it.*

"You are so beautiful, Pan Dora," Asia said. "Are you a Goddess?"

Pan Dora looked confused to Asia. Despite being over 40, she was still a beautiful woman. She understood Asia thanks to the microchip implanted within her brain. It helped her to understand and speak the language of Greecee quite perfectly.

Pan Dora, moved closer to Asia and spoke softly so Pea couldn't hear her. "Did you tell him who his father is?"

"Yes," Asia smiled. "I have nothing to hide. He knows his father is Prometheus." She was silent for a little while. Tears of nostalgia welled in her eyes. "It has been more than twenty years since I heard anything from him." She tried to brush her tears away with the bank of her palm. "Why he would care about me now? I am old. Too old."

"Don't speak like that Asia. Prom—Prometheus—is special. He's different than the others. He had his differences with Zeu and that's why he sent me here," Pan Dora paused. "He told me to teach his son how to become a good doctor. Like his father." At this, Pan Dora rose and looked down warmly at Asia, "And I will do just that."

For a long moment the two ladies gazed at each other in silence. Then, casting her eyes to the other side of the room, Asia said, "That box ... what did you bring us in that box? I know you have diamonds. We are poor. I don't want my son to be poor. If Prometheus sent you with diamonds for us, we are in great need."

"There are no diamonds in the box Asia," Pan Dora warned.

"But ... what's in it then?"

"Pain, suffering, tears, and death!" Pan Dora moved back next to Asia, "Please promise me you will never open the box."

Asia looked at her, confused.

"As I said," Pan Dora continued, "I will teach Pea the art of medicine, and it won't be long before he is rich and famous. You will have a nice life as rich lady, Asia. But please: promise me you will never open the box. Promise me."

"I – I promise ..." Asia said, trying to appear serious.

The next day, Pan Dora invited the young man Pea to join her for a walk. Walking in silence with Pea, she had a look around her at the island. It appeared to be quite large, but in fact it was a medium to small-sized island compared to others on the planet. Far away in the distance, she saw another piece of land. She knew that if the box were to be opened, the virus would easily spread to the other islands and from there, to the continent.

The people of the island were mostly peaceful. They dressed mainly in white robes, which suited the climate, which was hot in the summer, despite the sea breezes. There were some warriors who wore light amour and carried swords, but the majority of the people were peaceful and respectful. Discreetly they watched Pan Dora and Pea as they walked. She knew this was normal, as she was the most beautiful woman on the island. There were other nice looking girls and women on the island, but none so perfect as Pan Dora.

"Did your mother tell you about your father?" Pan Dora asked with a kind smile at Pea.

"Yes. She said he is a god, and that he lives on Mount Olympus."

Pan Dora smiled to herself. *They must have noticed the temporary base we had at the top of the mountain they call Olympus.*

"Yes, he is a god of Olympus, but than that, he is a great doctor. I have heard that you also love medicine. Your mother told me about your passion," She stopped walking and turned to look seriously at Pea.

"It's true, I have a great passion for medicine," he seemed embarrassed to talk about himself, and avoided her eyes.

For a moment they stood in silence, watching a small group of children playing nearby.

"What I don't understand," Pea continued, "is why he never bothered to meet me, or even to give me a book about medicine."

"He was not permitted to." Pan Dora replied firmly. "But he sent me here instead."

"To marry me?" Pea hazarded a guess.

Pan Dora smiled at him with regret. "Unfortunately not. He sent me here to teach you medicine. And I will. I'll teach you about the miraculous substances contained within each healing plant. I'll teach you how to separate and distill them. I'll teach you how to create medicine from them. And how to use that medicine to cure people." She stopped and gestured at a delicate white flower, "For example, do you know this plant?"

"Yes, we call it chamomile."

"Correct." Pan Dora said, "but I noticed you don't use

it often, and you don't know it's medicinal properties. Dem created it especially for you--" Pan Dora cut herself off before she could say, '*in her genetic mutation laboratories.*'

"Dem? You mean Demeter, the Goddess of agriculture?"

"Yes," Pan Dora smiled at him, but she stopped talking as a little girl approached her.

Politely the little girl smiled to Pan Dora and addressed her in a tiny voice, "Hello, My name is Maria. What's your name, pretty lady?"

Pan Dora bent down to the little girl. "My name is Pan Dora," she replied kindly.

The blue-eyed girl was dressed in a short robe, and beautiful golden hair tumbled over her shoulders.

"You are very beautiful, Pan Dora," the little girl said, with obvious admiration.

"Thank you Maria. You are beautiful too. Soon you'll be a nice young lady like me."

Pan Dora smiled again at the little girl, and her smile froze on her face. *If you are lucky enough to live that long, Maria.*

Pan Dora shook her head and continued on her walk with Pea. In time, they reached top of a little hill, and she turned to her companion, "We need garlic, honey, vinegar made from apples, and few other minor ingredients. I hope we can find a cold cavern on this island where we can mix these ingredients and leave them for a time to steep. I'm going to teach you how to brew a very powerful medicine that can kill the most powerful virus or bacteria. We need to mix all these ingredients together, and leave them to soften and soak in a cold place for at least a week. Two would be better. After that, we will need to filter it, and then it should be ready to go. Then it will be ready to be administered to affected people."

Pea looked confused; he didn't understand her urgency. "And what's the name of this medicine you want to teach me to prepare?"

"Let's call it an antibiotic. And we may need it very soon. "On their way back to the village, they talked at length about the preparation of the garlic-based remedy.

When they arrived back at Pea's home, a cold sensation descended on Pan Dora.

"Asia! You—you opened the box! I told you not to open it!"

"I'm sorry, my dear ... so very sorry ... I was just so curious, you see. I thought there might be something valuable inside. But it was nothing but an empty box. No diamonds..." Asia paused and looked around, confused. "I feel bad, Pan Dora, like a fever might be coming on..."

"I know," Pan Dora replied sadly, in a low voice. "That box was not as empty as you thought."

For a moment, Pan Dora felt paralyzed by the all of the possible consequences she could foresee. But she knew she had to think quickly, *I don't have the luxury to wait now. I have to act quickly.* She watched Pea gently touch his mother's cheek.

"She has a fever," he said looking up at Pan Dora. "What does this mean?"

"It means we no time to waste. We have to prepare the antibiotic immediately."

"Look at that whore!" Zeus shouted.

He was seated with Herr on a floating platform far away above the island. The platform was shielded from sight by an invisibility device, which meant that they couldn't be seen from the island with the naked eye. Herr was still a little bit confused about Zeu's choice to observe his plan unfold unseen. He – and the others, for that matter – didn't usually hesitate to show themselves to the earthlings. *And yet he cares so much about secrecy now. Why, I wonder?* However, she didn't bother to ask Zeu about his new interest in being invisible.

From the floating platform, the two could see down to the island clearly thanks to a view amplifier. Herr was enjoying the beautiful scenery of the vibrantly blue sea and sky, and the brilliantly yellow sun. Even the island appeared pretty to her, despite the fact Herr was not normally an admirer of islands. She tended to prefer the larger feudal cities. This island was only a collection of a few villages, and not entirely to her taste.

"What a fucking whore!" Zeu repeated, even more loudly than before. Through the view amplifier they could now see Pandora working frantically to build a rudimentary distillation device.

"She was supposed to stay there and suffer! To watch all those people die in terrible conditions. She was supposed to spend every minute of her time here on this island in pain! She should have been overcome by the stink of rotten human bodies by now. Instead, she tries to help them!"

"Anyone in her place would do the same," Herr said in a calm voice.

"No!" Zeu roared. "My plan was for her to observe only. Now she will stay on this dirty island hundreds of years."

"I'd imagine you want to resign from this mandate," Her said looking down at the island dispassionately.

Zeu turned to her, an expression of profound hunger distorting his features.

As though she saw nothing, Herr continued, "According to the current regulations, no one is allowed to stay on the planet, in a populated area, more than three terrestrial months."

"I will extend it to four on this particular case," he said, turning back to the view amplifier. He struggled to appear calm.

"Well … you may be the current leader of this project, but the real control belongs to Dem and Hest. And you know that very well."

Studying as events unfolded on the island, Zeu said, "I will have a meeting with them in two hours, and I will fix that too."

Herr let out a short burst of laughter. "Good luck with that," she chuckled, and continued to admire the beautiful view. "I should think that you wouldn't want to extend her time on the planet, since she is teaching Prom's son about antibiotics, medicinal plants and the fundamentals of medicine. The longer she is there, the more knowledge she will pass on to the inhabitants. She is a superior citizen of our ship and our world. Her IQ is very high."

Ignoring Herr's sarcasm, Zeu wondered aloud, "Do you think she'll be successful with that crude antibiotic?" He turned toward Herr and watched her with interest.

She smiled at him. "I'm not entirely sure. The virus

I put in the box belongs to a very aggressive strain. She paused to add impact to her next words, "I do think it will be extremely interesting to watch the live show, however. I am curious myself."

—————— ⚬ ——————

The villagers from the little sunny island looked different now. It had only been five days since the box was opened, but the plague had spread across the island. Everyone was covered in ugly, blue-black bruises. Everybody that is, except Pan Dora. It appeared she was immune to this particular virus after all. *At least Zeu didn't dare to take that risk,* she thought.

At a young age, Pan Dora's crystalline eyes had been replaced by powerful bionic lenses. These lenses were connected to the microchip implanted in her brain. She was quite sure that Zeu was watching everything, through her eyes, in three dimensions in one of the projection rooms. Through the lens she was able to amplify the images and, through the microchip implanted in her brain, to view and analyze them. She was thus able to watch the virus's development live. She now knew each and every molecule and atom in its composition. She hated each and every one of them for causing so much suffering.

The people were nearing the final phase of the illness: death. *So much pain, so much suffering,* she thought. *The only one who is happy is the virus.* Pan Dora watched as the virus branched out and spread, feeding happily on the blood of the island's habitants. *You can be sure Herr is also happily watching these live images on the ship,* she revised her earlier observation. And yet, Pan Dora still didn't damn Herr. *She did this to advance the science of sickness.* She worked to recreate complicated biochemical reactions in her mind as she tried to determine the projected molecule of the garlic-based antibiotic.

After that, she took a sample of healthy virus and put it together with the antibiotic inher mind. On the mental projection, the virus shrank, became week, and finally perished. Pan Dora felt quite happy for the first time in days. *It is an optimistic projection.*

She looked over at Pea. He was also suffering. His body looked terrible. She kept trying to continue his intense medical training sessions, but as his body become weaker and weaker, she decided it was time to stop.

"Pan Dora," begged Pea, "we have to start administrating your antibiotic to the people."

"Not yet," Pan Dora said firmly. "The maceration and fermentation process is not complete yet. I told you, we needed at least a week for it to distill. Then, we have to filter it and only then can we give it to the people."

"They're dying, Pan Dora. They need it today," Pea tried to muster the strength to convince her, but his moribund voice betrayed him. "It should be concentrated enough by now."

"No." Pan Dora kept her voice firm. "The antibiotic is still too dilute. The distillation process is not done yet. If we were to use it now, it is highly probable we'd be wasting it." She paused to look at him with compassion. "And I can't take that risk."

"The people will die. I will die too."

"Some people will die, that's unavoidable I'm afraid; but not you. I won't let you die."

———————◇———————

The next day as she walked around the island, Pan Dora was shocked at how dramatically the situation had worsened overnight. So far there were at least thirty casualties, mainly the elderly, but she knew it would get worse before it got better. As she walked, she realized she was standing in front of little Maria's house. She decided to go inside. Maria, her parents, and her three brothers were lying in their beds in terrible suffering. Maria's grandmother had been one of the casualties yesterday, and two men were removing her body to take to the common burial pit at the edge of the village. Pan Dora had insisted that the village prepare in this manner.

Little Maria looked extremely bad. Her entire body was covered in bruises, and it was clear she was in the throes of death. With her dying eyes, she looked at Pan Dora. She had no energy to talk, but she mouthed Pan Dora's name soundlessly.

It broke Pan Dora's heart.

"Look at me Maria. You will be healthy very soon. You won't die. I will not let you die. There is hope for you. You have to hope." She lightly touched the little girl's forehead head. She had a very high fever. "I will be back, Maria. Hold on for me."

Pan Dora rushed to the bottom of the cold cavern where she had stashed the vessels with the garlic-based antibiotic six days ago. With a stick, she stirred the contents of the vessels, to blend the liquid into a homogeneous mixture.

Using a clean piece of cotton, she filtered several spoonfuls of the fluid.

She covered the little vessel containing the newly filtered antibiotic and rushed quickly back to Maria. She placed her a tiny spoonful of the antibiotic on her lips. The little girl coughed at the bitter taste of the elixir. Pan Dora gave her plenty of water to drink and went back to Pea's house. She gave him some of the antibiotic as well. She tried to support him to stand up, but it was too big of an effort for him. Outside, the weather was beautiful. It was a beautiful warm evening. Pan Dora intended to sleep close by Pea, but the liquid oozing out of his bruises nearly made her vomit.

She decided instead to sleep outside under the clear blue sky. The sky was so beautiful, so full of stars. *Somewhere out there is my home planet. My home that I've never seen*, Pan Dora mused. *And somewhere out there is the ship.* She knew it would be far enough from the planet that it wouldn't be possible to be seen by the naked eye. Pan Dora hated the fact that Zeu was looking down on her from there.

She had no idea when she felt asleep, but she woke to birdsong and a beautiful morning. As soon as she arose, Pan Dora rushed up to little Maria's house. The girl was sleeping deeply, and Pan Dora gently touched her forehead. Her fever had decreased.

My antibiotic works!

Pan Dora felt the sting of tears springing to her eyes. She knew she must keep herself under control, however, as there was still an immense amount of work to be done. The antibiotic would have to be administrated to all the people in the village. And she would need to ensure she had prepared enough of it in the vessels at the cave.

She paused a moment to smile at the beautiful child's face. Despite the fact that the little girl was sleeping and couldn't hear her, Pan Dora bent close to her and said, "like I told you Maria, there is hope."

***

Herr and Zeu were in the large office by the full-length window. They had been arguing for over half an hour, but were now taking a break to look down at the planet. Herr decided to keep quiet a moment longer to allow Zeu to calm down. They stood together in silence, admiring the beautiful blue ball. *I can't be angry at the planet,* Herr reflected, *it remains a thing of beauty despite our feud. At least, that's what I think. Zeu on the other hand – he might be thinking of his mistress down there on the planet. Or one of his many bustards.* This possibility made her suddenly furious. There had been many times by now that she was not able to control herself when thoughts of Zeu's sexual adventures flooded her mind. When that happened, she was not herself. She acted cruelly. She knew Zeu psychological profile very well. She smiled to herself at the thought: *I know him better than he knows himself.*

She turned to him and said, "you have to let me to bring her back! Discordia is awaiting my decision."

With a nervous gesture, Zeu turned from the window and stalked to the middle of the room. "No!" He bellowed, full of fury. "I said no!"

Herr was pleased with his reaction, for she intended to bring him to the threshold of his madness and cruelly play with him. "You're acting foolish. Article 121 of the Ship and Planet Rules and Regulations allows no one to spend more than 90 consecutive days on the planet. You failed to convince Dem and Hest to extend this term for Pan Dora. Therefore, today is her last allowable day on the planet," she finished, her voice very convincing. "We have to bring her back within the hour. Otherwise, you face terrible consequences." She accentuated the last words. Finally she continued, "Even you aren't above the law, Zeu."

Zeu was walking in nervous circles around the room. "Then I will change the Ship and Planet Rules and Regulations," he ranted. "I don't want her beak!" Zeu was screaming now.

It took effort for Herr to hide a large grin. She continued in an a consoling voice, "I thought you were mature enough to understand and accept that there are things beyond even your control."

He stalked toward her angrily. Herr remained calm. She was prepared for him to hit her, and she tried to keep herself calm. "As I said, I can't watch you destroy your entire career because of Pan Dora. I can't let my reputation as your first advisor be affected by a stupid decision like this." She raised her voice to him now.

He stepped angrily toward her, but she turned her back toward him and she said in a voice as strong as steel:

"Discordia, please use the ship teleportation's features to bring back Pan Dora."

When Pan Dora woke up in the teleportation room, nobody was there waiting for her. The white, wall-less room was completely empty. She appeared to be alone in the middle of a white universe. For a moment, she felt more depressed than she had been down on the Planet. *All that effort was for nothing?*

Her chest felt like it would burst from sobbing.

But at that moment, someone materialized in the teleporter. Student Number 13 appeared near her. He was dressed in a white robe. Despite his long white beard and hair, he the same as the last time she had seen him; handsome, with a nicely muscled body. He had a large smile on his face, and he was holding a lovely bouquet of white flowers. Very special flowers, formed from a single petal. He knew they were called Calla and that they were Pan Dora's favorites.

He hugged Pan Dora and he offered her the bouquet.

"You are so brave, Pan Dora!"

"Thank you," she answered simply.

"Dem and Hest want to see you."

She smiled nicely, "I am sure they want to. I won't keep them waiting."

CHAPTER 20

War

What can be more exciting than a fight to death? What can be more exciting than war?

Arr – teaching the planet's inhabitants

Arr and Afronda were drenched in sweat after a lengthy and intensive sex session. Afronda was drinking a glass full of cold water, as she was very thirsty. While she quenched her thirst, Arr walked naked to the huge window overlooking the beautiful blue ball of the planet. He sent a mental command to the computer and the image zoomed in. Now, he could see the main continents. The image continued to zoom. It focused on the sea between Affra and Eurra. Naked, Afronda approached him, embracing him from behind.

"This sea is called Afronda's sea," she suggested coyly.

"I'm trying to be as polite as I can with you my love, but that is not the exactly name of the sea."

Afronda let go of him. She strode now toward the huge screen.

"But the people of Greecee think I was born out of the foam of the sea. Of *that* sea. That's why they call it by my name."

Arr gestured behind her. "I manipulated things like this because I don't want them to think I am one of Zeu's children."

Afronda continued to gaze at the huge screen that mainly showed Greecee with its many Islands.

"Like this, I am not ordinary." She paused to wait for the effects of her words, "Like you."

"Or him." Arr said from behind her, his face still registering disapproval. Afronda knew he was referring to Apoll.

Now the image drifted away from Greecee, out toward the sea until the next continent began to appear. A large, wonderful city appeared on the seashore. It was so big, it could be seen from the sky, without having to increase the magnification of the zoom.

"If we disregard the pyramids, this is the biggest construction on the earth at this point in time," Arr noted.

"It is indeed the biggest city built by the inhabitants of the planet," Afronda agreed. "And within it, you will find the biggest temple on the earth."

Now she turned toward Arr, "bigger than any of your temples, bigger than mine, bigger even than Zeu's or Athena's temples. In this massive temple, they pray to Apoll. How selfish he is!" Afronda said, disgusted.

"He claims his city is practically impenetrable," Arr said, ignoring Afronda's sarcasm. "However, I have chosen and specifically trained a human warrior. His name is Achill. I am confident he is the most highly-trained warrior on the earth," Arr was very convinced.

"This city – Trroy – has its own warrior prince," Afronda reminded him. "His name is Hecctor. Like you did with Achill, Arr trained Hecctor personally." She smiled delicately. "I've been told that in your bedroom fights, Apoll was even better than you, sometimes," she added, pausing just long enough stoke Arr's rage. "So the way I see it, because Apoll trained Hecctor, Hecctor might even be better than your Achill." Her remarks were also an accusation: *everyone on this ship knows about your gay relationship with Apoll.*

Arr smiled bitterly at Afronda, "As you say, he sometimes bested me in the bedroom. But even you know that real war is different. I suggest you leave this little detail to me."

"Well, if you didn't do a good enough job, you should be worried when Achill meets Hecctor in combat on the field of battle."

"I have no emotions about that!" Arr interrupted her abruptly, "You should be the worried one."

"Me?" she wondered. "Why should I worry?" Afronda asked in an irritated voice.

"So far your friend has done nothing; and our plan relies a great deal on it." Arr smiled bitterly at her.

"But she will act, and soon."

"Do you really trust her? Can you indeed manipulate her at that level?"

With a delicate gesture Afronda turned back to the huge screen that was showing the grateful city.

He might be wise in the art of war; otherwise he is quite naive.

Discordia bent her tall body down towards the young man, "You are a lovely young man, do you know that?"

"Thank you, my lady." Parriss, the young good looking boy in question, answered back. He knew he should return the compliment to Discordia, but she was not an attractive woman at all. She was too tall and too slim. Today she was dressed in a long white dress. Parriss couldn't figure out what kind of material her dress was made of. It fit absolutely tight to the woman's body. Because of this, she appeared even more tall and slim. However, despite her height and slimness, she walked normally. The material of her dress was so elastic, *we definitely don't have anything like that in our entire city or the nearby villages*, Parriss thought. *Not even in Greecee, regardless of how civilized they think they are.*

"We have been meeting for such long time now, my lady," Parriss said with respect. "I have learned so much from you. You are a wonderful teacher, and I am so very pleased. The knowledge you have given me has made me very respected in the city now. My brother Hecctor seeks my advice in everything."

"This is good," Discordia remarked gravely. "I think you are a clever young man, but..." And Discordia moved her eyes to the nearby arid field that surrounded the great city. She appeared to enjoy watching the shadow of city's external wall so much that she completely forgot what she was saying.

"But what, ma'am?" Parriss asked.

"Oh!" Discordia exclaimed, as though waking up from

a beautiful daydream. "I want you to improve your fighting skills too. At some point, your life may depend on it." She tried to offer a kind smile to the little prince.

"Despite the fact that you are a prince, someday you might end up standing alone in the front of one who might want to kill you, due to circumstances outside your control. And you should be skilled enough to defeat him."

"I will improve my fighting skills my lady. I promise." The young man tried to be convincing. "I am already very good in handling the bow and arrow."

"You are quite proficient with bow and arrows," Discordia agreed. "I saw you yesterday. All seven of your arrows hit the bull's-eye. I am so proud of you Parriss."

"You were around yesterday, my lady?" Parriss asked wonderingly.

"I don't need to be around to see you." Discordia stated gravely.

"It is true that you and the other gods can watch us from the top of Olympia mountain. Where is your castle?"

"It is true we can watch you. But, I'll share a little secret, just with you. Our castle is in the sky." *And we can watch you through our surveillance cameras*, Discordia completed the sentence in her mind.

"Oh!" The young man exclaimed, astonished.

Discordia left him to think a little while about this revelation. After a moment, she touched his shoulder in a friendly gesture. "Do not worry young Parriss. Here on earth, you live in the greatest city ever built. And you are its Prince. Not many people on the earth are lucky as you are. Therefore they will be resentful of your position." She paused. She took him by both shoulders and looked down into his beautiful young eyes.

"I want you to become more proficient in sword fighting. I had thought to find you a teacher, but I remembered that your brother Hecctor is a good swordsman. Ask him to teach you." She nodded toward him with conviction.

"I will my lady. You have my promise."

"It will be a great effort, but I am confident you will do your best."

"Yes my lady."

Discordia moved several steps away, as if to admire the dry fields again.

"However," she said without turning to look at him.

"However, what my lady?" Parriss asked intrigued.

"A good warrior needs sex," Discordia said simply.

"Wh-- what?" The young man was at a loss for words.

"I should broached this topic a little bit earlier, when we first began our meetings. But we had other priorities," She looked at him seriously. "I know you don't know too much about sex, but it is something that comes with practice," Discordia said very convincingly.

"Do you think so my lady?" Parriss was a bit embarrassed.

"Yes. And as a Prince, you aren't required to wait until you get married. So, who would you like to have sex with first?" She asked him in a normal voice. "Obviously not with me. I am your mentor, and not as pretty as Afronda."

The young man remained speechless.

"Afronda is not only beautiful, she is also sexually ... talented. And ..." Discordia paused, gazing him, "... here she is."

Now Discordia looked at a point beyond Parriss's

shoulder. Confused, Parriss looked back. And indeed, there stood Afronda herself. She was even more beautiful in real life than the statues or pictures that tried to imitate her. She wore a nice white dress in a light fabric that was just transparent enough for him to make out the shape of her wonderful body.

Afronda smiled indulgently at him. *It's no wonder he's so confused; it's impossible for him to understand our teleportation capabilities.*

Parriss watched her in astonishment. As though in a dream, he heard Discordia's words from behind him.

"I will watch to make sure nobody disturbs you. You can spend as much time as you need together."

Saying this, Discordia walked away. She mentally checked the images from nearby floating cameras, to ensure nobody else was nearby.

With delicate gestures, Afronda removed her dress. Now she stood naked in front of Parriss. With easy grace, she stepped toward him and undressed him.

Back on the ship, Discordia walked the length of the control room. Her two operators watched holographic projections of the ballroom. When John realized that Discordia was behind him, he tried to quickly close the holographic projection showing the list of invited guests.

"You can check it," Discordia said in her tiny voice. "It's no secret that he invited everybody but me." She appeared quite sad. "After so many millennia, this guy still doesn't understand that I'm a part of senior management."

"This is true, ma'am. And unfair," Emm tried to console her. "Quite unpredictable."

"Unpredictable, maybe," Discordia continued in her sad voice. She walked close to Emm, "But not for me. And he will pay for this." She paused and changed her tone of voice, "And his beloved city will pay along with him."

"The party will start very soon my Prince," a nice young man announced and then promptly exited the room, leaving Parriss alone. Parriss did not even turn to acknowledge him.

He realized that he become dependent on sex. For the past two weeks, he had met Afronda almost daily. Everything went so nicely, so smoothly. Every night, before bedtime she just ... appeared, materializing from nothing in his bedroom. He knew the common people called her Aphrodite, the Goddess of Love. But to him, she was Afronda, the woman who had taught him the incredible allure of sex. He wished desperately for her to be here, in the room, right now. *But*, he reminded himself, *it is entirely possible she will be at the party.* He hated the idea that there would be so many people around and he would not be able to touch her.

"Ahem..." somebody nearby cleared their throat in a tiny voice. Somebody so familiar.

"Oh! My Lady! You're here." Parriss stood up instantly, and bowed to Discordia. "I am so happy you're here, my Lady!"

Discordia leaned her tall body towards him and she smiled as nice as she was able. "I am happy to see you too, my young prince."

For a moment, Parriss was confused, "There were some rumors that you … might not be able to attend the city's celebration."

"It is true," she moved her eyes to the room's ceiling, "that I was not invited," she spat the second part of the statement abruptly. "Apoll knows I am very busy in the sky castle, and he wanted to protect me." She looking down at Parriss again, trying to convince him. *What bullshit. I can't believe one word, but happily he is naïve.* Discordia thought. "But, I am sure *you* want me to attend the party," she finished aloud.

"Yes, of course ma'am," Parriss rushed to confirm. "You are my mentor – I owe you so much."

"True," Discordia acknowledged simply.

"Now," she paused, looking intensely down at him. "Now, I need you to help me with something."

"Anything, ma'am."

Discordia showed him her empty palm. Parriss looked at it, a little bit disappointed, but suddenly a golden apple materialized in her hand. For Parriss, this was unbelievable magic, but for Discordia, it was simple teleportation. Now Discordia smiled broadly. Emm had done a wonderful job teleporting the golden apple into her palm, at the precise coordinates she had just sent him.

Parriss was astonished by the beauty of the Golden Apple. He was certain the purity of the gold was very high, and the apple was perfectly made. Not a scratch was visible on its surface. *Everything about it is so perfect; a goddess made it*, Parriss thought.

"As I said," Discordia started with great importance, "I don't have much free time and I will leave the party shortly.

But before I leave, I will propose a little adult contest."
She smiled down at him. "I will make an announcement
and propose that you offer this golden apple to the most
beautiful woman in the room."

Parriss become suddenly excited. "Who could be more
beautiful than Afronda?" he wondered.

For a moment Discordia appeared as though she hadn't
heard him. "You may offer the apple to a goddess or a woman
from your city," she seemed to be daydreaming. "Oh—" she
continued, seeming surprised, "you said Afronda?"

"Yes ma'am," Parriss was quite excited now.

"Speaking of Afronda…" Discordia looked around the
room and then finally down at him. "This relationship with
Afronda cannot last forever. You know this."

"Yes ma'am." Parriss seemed devastated.

"But, I have good news." Discordia added in a happy
voice.

"Yes?" Parriss watched her with interest.

"Afronda has found a young woman on earth; one
almost as beautiful as her and … who shares her sexual
talents."

"Who is she ma'am?" Parriss was breathless.

"She will tell you her name tonight. After you give
her the golden apple. This will be one of your rewards."
Discordia nodded to him. "Shall we go now? The party
room should be full by now."

"Yes. Let's go."

It was as if the entire universe was moving around
him at high speed. He wanted so desperately to be near to
Afronda. She knew what he wanted. She knew every inch
of his body. She knew his sexual preferences perfectly. If she

had found a woman like herself, she would be perfect for him. It was like a dream.

In the front of the door a man was asking whom he should announce.

"You should announce Prince Parriss and the Goddess Discordia" She asserted firmly in her tiny voice.

The announcement was made. Parriss did not paying any attention to his surroundings, despite the fact that the room was full of people, gods and goddesses.

Discordia and Parriss wandered the huge party room for a time. Finally, Parriss heard Discordia addressing the room loudly. The room became silent, all eyes trained on Discordia.

She is such a smart woman, Parriss thought.

Finally he saw Afronda. He noticed she was looking toward the golden apple. Also, Athena, Herr, and several other Goddesses had gathered around, along with many beautiful girls from the city. Finally Discordia gave Parriss the golden Apple.

Immediately, Parriss was gave the golden apple to Afronda. She touched his fingers and leaned toward him. Finally, she whispered the name that he was so anxious to hear and know.

Ellen.

And with that, Parriss thought: *Ellen. I will make her Ellen of Trroy.*

CHAPTER 21

Management change

Good is good; bad is bad.

Thirteenth Student

Everything in the room was white. The table, the chairs, the walls. The leaders walked into the room one after the other. They were dressed in long white robes. Herm stood by the table and invited the leaders to take their seats around the table. Finally, they all took their seats. Zeu looked to the two seats at the head of the table.

"Dem and Hest wanted us to start this meeting without them," Herm said, still standing up by the table.

At once, the white walls surrounding the table dissolved to create a wall-less effect. Now the table was in the middle of a white universe. Suddenly, the table and began to shake up, a sensation that suggested great speed. The white universe disappeared and became blue. The table was now floating in a blue sky. With dizzying speed it zoomed toward Amerr. The table now hovered above the old continental mines.

The site was so massive, it could be seen form high above in the sky.

Etched into the top of the table, a sentence now appeared: *Our tracks here were supposed to be covered by now.* The sentence was highlighted in bold red letters.

With the same dizzying speed, the table raced next to the Assian continent. The cities here were pleasant, but in many places the people fought terribly. On the top of the table appeared the second sentence: *Too much violence.*

Suddenly the table sank deep into the ocean. Now they arrived at the submarine base. Around it swam large, terrible creatures. A third sentence appeared on the top of the table: *Unauthorized genetic experiments.'*

Swiftly the table surfaced and hovered above Trroy city, now almost destroyed. A new sentence appeared on the top of the table: *Massive destructive intervention in planet's politics.*

Suddenly the table became still and the white universe surrounded them again, returning a sense of calm to the atmosphere. Had it not been for the four blood red sentences flooding the table, it might have seemed like their short virtual reality travel around the planet had been nothing more than a bad memory.

Dem and Hest materialized in the two empty chairs.

"I can't believe how much you ladies influenced the events around Trroy," Zeu said, addressing an unhappy look to Dem and Hest.

"It's fair to say," Herr tried to maintain calm around the table, "that each of us has made mistakes."

"Not us," Hest said in a firm voice. "You can't compare our small interventions with your terrible mistakes."

"I merely taught them the basics of agriculture," Dem said in her normal and calm voice. "It was a really progressive and beneficial activity for the planet's habitants."

"And all I did was talk to some virgins," Hest said.

"All you did?" Poss questioned accusingly. "You also did genetic experiments in Ausstra. All the animals there look different from the rest of the planet. Those marsupials you created are very different to the animals from all the other continents.

"I don't think so," Hest argued in a remarkably calm voice. "Ausstra's marsupial animals might also be the result of the normal evolutionary process of earth under very isolated conditions. Ausstra is indeed a very isolated island continent. It will be very difficult for the humans to clearly prove it was a genetic modification when they have reached a high enough level of scientific sophistication."

Dem surveyed the table, "there should be solid boundaries in place regarding our interaction with the planet and its habitants."

"Enough is enough," Hest raised her voice and glared at Zeu.

"Okay," Athena said, "I'm sure we can fix this, if you give us a chance."

"We need to cover our tracks on the planet as much as we can." Dem said. "And it must be done in a very short time and remain unobserved by the planet's habitants."

"And why is that?" Discordia asked in her tiny voice.

Dem gestured to Herm, inviting him to speak.

"Because … we have finally established contact with our base." He was still standing beside the table.

A buzz of incredulous chatter arose from the leaders seated around the table.

"How is this possible, especially after such a long time?" Afronda was perplexed.

"A new technology. A combination of telepathy and radio communication," Herm explained. "However, it isn't possible for us to send large reports for now."

"Therefore still we have some time." Dem added.

"How quickly do you want this fixed?" Zeu asked in an upset voice.

"First of all I am not confident that you can handle this." Hest said abruptly, still smiling at him.

"What?" He demanded, banging his fist on the table.

Dem and Hest gazed at him dispassionately, "Your primary master until now has been the democratic system. We are not confident it will continue to be an effective form of governance. It is the time to replace democracy with technocracy. We need a more precise method of control than the one offered by democracy.

"Then who will coordinate the next stages?" Diane wondered.

"We asked our students to come up with innovative ideas," Dem said in a very calm and explanatory tone. "And one of them suggested a very agreeable proposal."

"Therefore, we have appointed him Absolute Leader," Hest announced smiling benevolently around the table.

For a moment the room was silent.

"As of this moment, not only Zeu, but each and every one of you are dismissed from your current leadership positions." Hest added.

Dem was smiled amiably.

"We will prepare positive reports regarding the activities of every one of you, but you are no longer permitted to interact with the planet's habitants, effective immediately. The main computer has already made the necessary software modifications and these prohibitions have already been implemented. You cannot fly or be teleported to the planet, starting now." Dem looked around the table. "The only exception is if the Absolute Leader is in need of someone's particular help, He has the authorization to ask the main computer to temporarily override some rules or a particular prohibition."

There was a long silent moment in the room.

"I guess… there is nothing too much to do or to say, as you have already decided this, ladies. Are you going to introduce us to this brilliant student?" Atena asked.

"Certainly," Hest smiled pleasantly around the table.

Suddenly a figure materialized beside the table trough teleportation.

"Student Number 13," Herr exclaimed.

"My previous name was Student Number 13. My current name is God. Please use my new name."

He seated himself in front of them and played with his white beard.

"Can you please briefly tell us about your project?" Dem asked.

God nodded approvingly to Dem and Hest. He stared to walk around the table. "In the first stage, some informative books will be prepared. They will teach people to be good. They will forbid crimes like incest, theft, and so on." As he was walking around the table, the ex-leaders eyed him carefully.

"During the second stage, Pan Dora will assist me closely. She will go to the planet and she will bring me a child. I chose her as she has a good planetary experience already. Our child will implement new teachings and he will bring light in the world."

Athena stood up and strode toward him.

"Good luck to you, God. It is a brilliant project. If you need our help, we will be happy to assist you."

She shook his hand. The other leaders followed her example and stood to congratulate him.

"This meeting is adjourned," Dem announced.

LIST OF MAIN CHARACTERS

The below characters are the products of careful genetic selection. As a result, they are all very intelligent. Their lifespans have been extended to eternity due to their advanced technology. They are well trained and they have large experience in all domains.

Supreme leaders:

Uran   *Supreme Leader of the mission.* He has overdeveloped muscles, dark short hair, white skin, and dark eyes.

Gee   *Uran's deputy.* She is a beautiful woman, with a well-muscled body, long dark curly hair, and green eyes.

Cronn   *Uran's deputy.* He has overdeveloped muscles, short dark hair, white skin, and dark eyes.

Zeu   *Second Supreme Leader of the mission.* His muscles are even more developed than the muscles of the others men. His long black hair extends past his shoulders. He has a long black beard, tanned skin, and black eyes

| **Herr** | *Zeu's deputy.* Her body is maybe a little bit too muscled for a woman. She has white skin, black long curly hair, and green eyes. |

Representatives of the Owners:

| **Dem** | A mature-looking woman, medium in height to tall, with a beautiful face, black hair with some white streaks, and black eyes. |
| **Hest** | A youthful-looking woman with beautiful black short hair and hazel eyes. |

Leaders:

Herm	*Ship's Captain.* He has a beautiful body with white skin, dark short hair, and blue eyes.
Heff	*Ship's Mechanical Officer.* He is ugly, fat and deformed. He has short dark hair, dark skin, and dark eyes.
Poss	*Chemist.* He has a muscled body, with black hair, light tanned skin, and blue eyes.
Apoll	*Software Engineer.* He has a very beautiful body, white skin, long blond curly hair, and blue eyes.
Prom	*Ship's Doctor.* He is massively muscled, but tall and well-proportioned. He has quite long black hair, white skin, and green eyes.
Arr	*Chief Security Officer.* He has overdeveloped muscles, long dark curly hair, white skin, and dark eyes.

Athena   *Strategist.* She has a beautifully muscled body, white skin, black hair, and black eyes.

Afronda   *Beauty Representative.* She is an extremely beautiful woman with very white skin, long blond curly hair, and blue eyes.

Discordia *Control Room Leader.* She is extremely tall and thin, with almost alien-like proportions. She has white skin, very short black hair, and dark eyes.

Discordia and her two Control Room Operators belong to the first generations, when genetic selection technology was less advanced.

Printed in the United States
by Baker & Taylor Publisher Services